Life After Sunday

By Sheritha Bowman

Copyright © 2010 by Sheritha Bowman

All rights reserved. No part of this book shall be reproduced or transmitted in any form or by any means, electronic, mechanical, magnetic, photographic including photocopying, recording or by any information storage and retrieval system, without prior written permission of the publisher. No patent liability is assumed with respect to the use of the information contained herein. Although every precaution has been taken in the preparation of this book, the publisher and author assume no responsibility for errors or omissions. Neither is any liability assumed for damages resulting from the use of the information contained herein.

This is a work of fiction. Names, characters, places, and incidents either are the product of the author's imagination or are used fictitiously. Any resemblance to actual events or locales or persons, living or dead, is entirely coincidental.

ISBN 0-7414-5805-5

Published by:
INFI∞ITY
PUBLISHING.COM
1094 New DeHaven Street, Suite 100
West Conshohocken, PA 19428-2713
Info@buybooksontheweb.com
www.buybooksontheweb.com
Toll-free (877) BUY BOOK
Local Phone (610) 941-9999
Fax (610) 941-9959

Printed in the United States of America
Published January 2010

CHAPTER ONE
Tyanne

Sunday, February 14, 1993

I am so not listening to this sermon. If Pastor Murphy could read my thoughts, he would probably, ask me to get my things, my four fidgety kids and get to stepping. I wouldn't blame him. Aside from shouting an occasional amen and hallelujah, I'm just sitting here taking up space because I haven't heard a word Pastor has preached all morning. All I can think about is how I'm going to tell my husband Marcus that I'm leaving him this weekend.

My best friend Patrice tells me I spend too much time complaining and not enough time praying and fasting for my husband's salvation. I mean, that's easy for her to say especially when her husband comes in here every Sunday jumping up and down and shouting about to rip his blazer. Don't get me wrong, I'm glad everything has worked out between Patrice and Melvin. I remember the days when she was hoping right along with me for her man to get his stuff together. Now Melvin, excuse me, Deacon Melvin is now saved, Holy Ghost filled and fire baptized. Praise ye the Lord. But Lord knows my concerns are beyond just wanting Marcus to get saved. I'm a minister. My husband is a drug dealer.

Marcus says he's not dealing anymore. I don't believe him. I believe he's slipped back into his old ways. Ways that I will not and cannot tolerate as a God-fearing, minister of the gospel. It was commitment, the anointing and my Mary J. Blige sounding voice that has earned me the position of assistant minister of music at Solid Rock Christian Center. I've been known to slay folk in the aisles on Sunday mornings whenever I open my mouth to sing. Not a boast, just a testament to the blessings and power of God. Something I praise God for each and every day.

"Mommy, I gotta go to the bathroom," Jordan, my three year old says as he pulls on my hand and snaps me back into the sermon. Without any idea of what Pastor Murphy is talking about, I shout 'amen.' The least I can do is pretend I'm paying attention. *God forgive me.*

Even if I was trying to hear the sermon, I can't because Jordan has asked to go to the bathroom at least a billion times already and then when we get there he says he doesn't have to go anymore. It's either take him or spend unnecessary money on Pull Ups and just let him pee himself forever. So we play the 'I *really* gotta go to the bathroom this time Mommy' game. I've already taken him a few times, so this time I nod and mouth to Tiffany, my moody sixteen year-old for her to take him.

She smacks her lips so hard I almost pop her on the back of her neck. Instead I just give her "the look" and she fixes her face. Tiffany would rather pluck her eyeballs than take Jordan to the bathroom in the middle of church service. As I stare at Tiffany, I see me and Marcus all wrapped up as one. She has Marcus' honey colored skin and my heart shaped face. Her body is maturing a little too fast for me, but she can't help it. I got all my stuff at her age, too.

Aunt Ruby, my mother's sister, is sitting with us and gives me an angry look for not moving forward with the popping on the back of the neck. She hasn't said anything, but I'm all too familiar with her constipated facial expression. Aunt Ruby tells me I let the kids smack their lips too much. She says if they were her kids she would smack their lips on the floor. I respect Aunt Ruby, but I'm really trying to get away from popping the kids every time they do something I don't like.

"Mommy, I'll take him." Summer, one of my eight year-old twins offers in a voice she believes is a whisper, but is far from it. This time I'm certain that I see Pastor Murphy look in our direction. This is embarrassing.

Patrice, who is sitting up in the front with her fine man of God and two well-behaved kids, peeps back at me several times. She's trying not to laugh at my obvious frustration. I want to choke her. Usually, all the kids are in their youth classes and I would be sitting up in the front row along with the rest of the ministerial staff, however today is Family Day. We have a guest choir and church members are encouraged to sit with their families. So here I sit with Aunt Ruby and my four kids. A part of me wishes that Marcus were here and the other half of me knows I'm better off not having to deal with him nodding off and falling asleep.

"Shhh, not so loud," I say to Summer, "Tiffany will take him." Summer pouts as she believes she is the second Mommy of the family and has been denied her parental rights. I can't help but laugh to myself as I see that little forehead of hers scrunch up. Summer takes after me with her cocoa skin and high cheek bones. Jordan has the chunky cheeks and the eyes that just about disappear when he smiles.

I place Jordan's hand into Tiffany's. Marcus, Jr., Summer's twin, pauses a moment from doodling some crazy looking action figures on the church program to take in what we're doing. Although Lil' Markie (we like to call him) looks identical to Summer, he's the spitting image of his father. Usually he's drumming or tossing and turning in his seat, so this is a blessed reprieve. I catch the eye of one of the ushers who is obviously displeased with Lil' Markie's defacement of the church program. At least he's quiet. Doodle away baby. I want to snap at the usher sarcastically and tell her to take it out of my tithes if she wants, but I know it's just the frustration getting to me over this whole situation with Marcus.

Things haven't been the same between us since those masked men came into the apartment and nearly killed me and the children. It's been about seven years ago, but I remember it as if it happened yesterday. I was pregnant with the twins at the time and Tiffany was about eight or nine. I was asleep when I heard this loud boom. I jumped up in bed to gather my thoughts, trying to determine if the noise I heard was part of my dream or reality. No sooner than I look over to check on Tiffany who is lying next to me, I hear footsteps like galloping horses coming toward the bedroom. There are strangers in my home.

Just as I start to get out of bed, two masked men dressed in black snow suits burst into the bedroom. One of them covers my mouth with his black leather glove and pulls me from bed. He asks me where the money is as he holds a gun at the temple of my head. I tell him it's in the other room. The other guy is pacing back and forth while Tiffany is crying and screaming. Real TV stuff. I'd heard stories, but never in a million years would I have imagined that I would be the one to experience it. My heart is pounding so hard I think I'm going to pass out. My whole body is trembling as he walks me to the other bedroom where the money is hidden.

With the gun still pointed at my temple, I reach into the corner of the dresser drawer and pull out stacks of money tied in rubber bands. All of the drug money Marcus has saved up, every dollar, I hand it over. He then asks for the rest of the money. I tell him that's all there is. It's the truth. I gave him all I knew about. He didn't believe me. He starts yelling and getting rougher with me demanding that I give him the rest of the money. I start praying aloud asking God to help me, to save me. I don't want to die. Not this way. Not over drug money. The gunman yells to his partner who is in the other room to take the money and go to the car. He grabs it and runs out of the door. The gunman yells at Tiffany and tells her to sit on the bed. I tell her its okay and to do what he says. He then pushes me and tells me to bend down as he turns me away from him and tries to push my face down into the bed. I struggle and do all I can to stop him from forcing me down. I had a feeling this would be the position he would use to shoot me, cold bloodied in the back of the head right in front of my daughter. I grab my stomach and I begin wailing as if I am going into labor. I don't know where the thought came from to fake labor, but I did it. There was no pain. At least not in my stomach; surviving the moment was all that mattered to me. I needed to save me and my children. I would try what I could to gain his sympathy and only hope God would spare my life and the lives of my children.

I kept moaning and groaning. Holding my stomach and keeping my body upright, I was determined not to surrender to the bent down position. I fight for all I'm worth. Seems the gunman had a change of heart. He told me to sit in the chair, shut up and not to move unless he would kill me.

He begins backing out of the room to leave, still pointing the gun in my direction. I hear the door slam, but I dare move. Soon I hear nothing but the cold air that is whistling through the bullet busted balcony glass door. Tiffany is sitting on the bed taking in quick breaths, staring at me with her eyes big as day. I begin to loose my arms and legs from the ties, all the while thanking Jesus over and over. I put on a coat over my gown, slide into my slippers, wrap Tiffany in her coat, get in the car and drive to Aunt Ruby's house.

God saved me, my daughter and my unborn babies that night. God is so merciful and gracious. He didn't have to spare my life or that of my children, but He did. There was no way things could go back to the way they were. I could no longer go on living life as a hustler's wife.

I was sure Marcus would pull out of the game for good after that. But all it did was make him hustle even harder. He said he wanted to replace the money that was stolen. I couldn't believe it. Yet he promised me that he would pull out just as soon as he replaced every dollar that was stolen. In the meantime, I was a walking, paranoid basket case.

Although Marcus moved us into a new home in the suburbs, installed an alarm system and put a secured gate on our front door, I never felt safe. Wherever I went, I was forever looking behind my back fearing those masked men would come back again. Who was to say they wouldn't? They knew who we were but we had no idea who they were. I told Marcus the name I believed I heard that night, but he said he had no idea who it was. Marcus suspected any and everybody, which didn't help to comfort me at all.

For months after that, my physical and mental health took a toll. I experienced excruciating stomach pains and anxiety attacks where I would jump up screaming out of my sleep and my heart would beat so fast I believed I would have a heart attack. The fear was driving me crazy. I was forever complaining about hearing noises and would get out of bed no less than a dozen times to look out of the window before falling asleep at night.

Not to mention the stress on our marriage. Marcus and I were constantly yelling and screaming at the top of our lungs about him never being home, him never taking me out, and about him coming off the streets. He would always remind me that I knew he was a hustler when I met him and I never had anything to say when he was spending the money on my clothes and hair.

Usually after every argument, he would just walk out, slam the door and drive to the city leaving me alone with the kids; kids who deserved at least one parent who could be there for them emotionally. I didn't have it to give. I needed a release. And the release I chose was to yell at the kids. No matter what they did, it always annoyed me. I would yell at them, they would start to cry and then I would cry because I made them cry. Every now and then to make myself feel better, I would convince myself that the answer to my problems would be to pack up the kids and move to Aruba or some island where no one knew me. Once I got there, my plan would be to lie on the beach all day, let the kids run around, and once my money ran out, I would sing for food.

Singing is my gift; my therapy.

On those lonely days and nights when the fear and depression tried and consume me, I just closed my eyes and began to hum, sing, scat - whatever my heart felt. With tears streaming down my face, I'd begin to hum a song of my heart's creation unto the Lord. From singing to scatting and imitating the voices of my favorite women jazz vocalists like Cassandra Wilson, Dianne Reeves, and Nancy Wilson. Those women jazz pioneers, who are able to make their voices roar and rumble with soothing sounds that come from the center of their hearts. I too, would sing a love song, a song of salvation, a song that will allow me to release all of the hurt and pain that was buried deep on the inside.

Until recently, I had grown all too content in accepting that my jazz originals would only be heard by God's angels and the walls of my home. That was until Nile Rivers, our minister of music, approached me. Nile plays the keyboard for our church on Sundays and spends the rest of the time gigging jazz concerts locally and nationally. He called me in for an audition and right on the spot he offered me the opportunity to do the vocals on his upcoming debut Christian jazz CD. Excited ain't even the word. I screamed and hugged Nile so hard his glasses fell off. This would be the dream of a lifetime. Not only are we cutting a CD, the church will host its very first CD release concert on Wednesday. We've contacted all of the local media outlets and it has fast become the talk of DC.

I told Marcus about it, looking for him to get just a little excited, and all I got from him was, "That's nice baby" and then within a millisecond he asked me if anybody had called him. I was too through. I bet if I told him I was collaborating with Jodeci or Keith Sweat, he would be all up in my face. I just decided I wouldn't bring it up again. And neither has he. So I'm sure he has totally forgotten about the big CD release party and will tell me he has to be at Champions on Wednesday.

Champions is a very successful nightclub that Marcus owns and I help to manage. It was something I encouraged him to do after the robbery to get off the streets before he was removed from the streets involuntarily. While I made decent money working as a full time administrative accountant for a law firm, Marcus laid low and started throwing hotel parties. He had already earned the nickname,

Marcus the Big Party Thrower. Whenever you heard talk of a happening party in town, you could always bet to hear Marcus' name. I convinced him to get his party business incorporated, publicize it and take it from the hotel ballrooms into a building of his own. And that's what he did. He took the money he saved from hustling and bought a nice little spot in downtown DC. Once an old blues nightclub, Marcus had it renovated, added his awesome gift of décor and named it Champions Restaurant & Nightclub.

He started off with deejays playing house music, DC go-go, R&B and whatever else that was hot on the radio. A few weekends a month we managed to book and feature some of the hottest R&B groups and rappers to perform live. As the audience grew, we brought in local talent and even started an amateur talent competition we call the "Hood Auditions" which features singers, poets, and comediennes. Every now and then, we have oldies but goodies nights where the grandmas and grandpas can get their groove on. I used my business savvy to hit up the local radio stations for heavy advertising to help make Champions one of the hottest and most popular nightclubs in the DC area.

Well, things are different now. I'm different now. My spirit has matured and my musical ear has changed. I can't stomach the environment at Champions anymore - the half-naked women, the alcohol, the drugs. I feel like a big hypocrite when I walk into church shouting hallelujah and just the other day I ordered ten cases of Remi Martin for the club. *Lord, have mercy.*

Although I don't attend the club, I'm still torn about managing it. The Christian lifestyle is about holiness and righteousness, everything that has to do with Champions is to the contrary.

I want so bad to take Champions to a whole new level that I've been having dreams about it. What I'd like to do is get some gospel and jazz music up in the house. Kirk Franklin, Fred Hammond, Kirk Whalum, Ben Tankard – they would go up in Champions and rock it out for Jesus. DC is growing hungrier and hungrier for gospel concerts and we have enough space to give them what they want. But of course Marcus doesn't want to hear any of this. I brought it up a few months ago, and we got into such a big argument about it that we didn't speak for two weeks. I just left it alone. But I can't keep quiet anymore. The compromising is killing me.

"Mommy, I went pee-pee and doo-doo." Jordan whispers in my ear ever so proudly as he and Tiffany return to their seats.

"Good job." I whisper back in my proud Mommy voice and kiss Jordan's cheek. Immediately he props himself on my lap, nestles his head into my bosom and closes his eyes. I press my cheek on top of his head and take in Jordan's fragrance of baby shampoo and coconut oil. Despite wanting to sometimes catch a one way flight to Aruba, God knows I love my children and there is nothing I wouldn't do for them.

"God has provided you with everything you need to make a change. Now, it's up to you ..." Pastor Murphy spoke as if he had entered my thoughts. He closed his Bible, signaling the benediction.

"I know that's the truth." I said softly gathering my things. Although my mind was made up, I'd have one last talk with Marcus tonight. I owed us that. Everything else I owed to God.

CHAPTER TWO
Marcus

"Man, please," I yell at Bone, "Holyfield will kick Mike Tyson's butt. He can come out of prison thinking he still reigns if he wants to. Holyfield got something for him." Mr. Freddie, my longtime barber jerks my head back into position as he tapers the sides of my hair. Mr. Freddie was old enough to be my father and had been cutting my hair from the sandbox. Had it been anybody else jerking my head like that, there would be a problem.

"Yeah, okay. You talking all that trash," Bone says with spit coming out of his mouth and half out of breath, "We'll see what happens when they finally meet up. And I will bet you five g's that Tyson will knock him out in the first round!"

Bone has asthma real bad. In the middle of a hyped conversation, he'll just start wheezing. But he'll keep right on wheezing and talking like nothing is happening.

"Bet?" I say as Bone walks up to me and clasps my hand in his to seal off our bet. Bone will defend Mike Tyson to his grave. Supposedly him and Mike are cousins. Bone be lying.

"I want my five thousand, too." Bone says as he squeezes all that tail into the barber chair to get a shape up.

I tell Bone all the time that he needs to lose some weight, but he's quick to cuss a brother out whenever you talk about his weight. I tell him it ain't just about losing weight for the women, it's about his health. Bone got to be about three hundred pounds easy. He's been big ever since third grade. That's how he got his name. Grown folks would always say he was big boned. The kids would just call him fat. But he'll tell you in a minute that he can still get the women whether he's fat or not. I guess he can. If I was a girl and a dude took me anywhere I wanted to go and gave me money to buy anything I wanted, I would fake like I was in love with him too. But that's my boy though.

Man. It's already five o'clock and I still haven't picked up anything for Tyanne for Valentine's Day. I tip Mr. Freddie, tell Bone I'll call him later and I do eighty around the beltway to the mall. Ain't no way I'm going home empty handed tonight. Especially not the way Tyanne has been acting lately.

Right now, Tyanne is into her monthly I'm-tired-of-you-not-going-to-church-and-I'm-tired-of-you-not-being-home bull. I've been real patient with her these last few months. I usually would have cussed her out by now. It's like she's been having her period for two months straight or something. So to keep from cussing her out, I've just been keeping my distance and spending more time at Champions or with Bone.

I've told that woman a million times the club can't run itself. How can I keep Champions in the number one spot if I'm always laying around at home? See Tyanne thinks I'm out here sleeping with all kinds of women and slinging dope. It's not even like that. But she has her mind made up that when I'm out late that's what I'm doing. She gets mad at me because them little simple chicks get our home number and play on the telephone. Or we might be out and some girl will walk up and start rapping with me and won't even acknowledge Tyanne. Of course I have to put them silly rabbits in check. I mean, I won't have them disrespecting my baby. Yea I admit. I used to mess around before we got married. Aw, man, I was a player. You better ask somebody. But that's not me anymore. I'm all about making money and taking care of my family now.

Now I won't lie and say that I won't look at a woman. Oh, I'm gonna look. But I know what these chicks are about. They can smell money a mile away. And they don't care if you're married with twenty kids, they gonna come at you. And they come at you hard. Some of these chicks that come into the club are unbelievable. Tits and butt hanging out everywhere; sticking their thongs and telephone number in your hand. Man, they make it hard for a brother. But see I know how far to go with these little hoochies. Yeah, I'll wink my eye at them every now and then. Give them a little compliment here and there. It's good for business. But that's as far as it goes. No chick out here comes close to what I have at home. I can get all the loving I want from my lil' Poo Poo at home. Plus, my baby looks good!

Besides that, I would never want to do anything to lose Tyanne. We've been through too much together. Tyanne was with me when I was driving my old raggedy, Impala with towels in the seats to cover the torn leather before I even had money. She has always been there for me. Truth be told, she nearly runs Champions. I stay out in the front and make the appearances while Tyanne runs everything behind the scenes. And she can handle her business. Tyanne is the one who got Champions that big write up in the Post a few summers ago. That's my baby. And the last thing I want to do is get involved with some chick and destroy what we have. I'll be the first to say that I'm truly a blessed brother. Let Tyanne tell it, I don't know how blessed I am. Oh, but I do.

I have what most Black men my age can only dream of having - a beautiful wife that's into church, four good-looking, healthy kids, a successful business, money flowing - I can't complain. Life is real good.

I sure have lots of company in Victoria's Secret. These brothers are walking around in the store like zombies looking for that last minute Valentine's gift. I bet half of them don't even know their woman's bra and panty sizes. That's a shame. You supposed to know everything about your woman. Even down to her underwear. Tyanne is a 36C cup, she wears medium underwear for that big booty and she wears a size eight in clothes. See brothers don't know their woman's size, because they don't buy them anything but on special holidays. I buy Tyanne pieces every chance I get. I like it when my baby looks good with her sexy self.

Since I waited until the last minute, everything is just about picked over. I grab a red teddy and a couple pair of thongs. I'll stop and get some yellow roses on the way home. The yellow roses alone usually put her in a good mood. Tyanne loves yellow roses.

"Marcus?"

I give the cashier my credit card and turn around to see who is calling my name. It's Phil Perry. Phil was the coke hook up when I was on the streets. Whenever we needed supply, we could count on Phil. He always had something to sell even when everybody else was dried out. The word on the street now is that Phil is into cruddy dealing. They say he's been beating brothers for their money and handing over tainted supplies. Not one to be trusted.

"Hey, what's up man?" I say as I lock into a brother handshake with him. "You waited until the last minute, too, huh?"

"Yeah, I just told her to pick out what she wanted." He says as he nods to this tall, light-skinned girl with oversized tits and a big flat pancake butt. I see her at Champions all the time with a different brother forever in her face. She's what you call an official freak body.

"I'm trying to get home to my wife before she changes the locks on me!" I say laughing as I pay for my stuff, grab my bag and head for the door.

Phil checks to see if he has my attention, pulls out a wad of twenties and hands them to Pancake Butt. I guess I'm supposed to be impressed.

"Hey, me and your boy been doing a little business lately. Did he tell you?" Phil says as he sneaks a quick peek at my shoes and pretends like he never looked. He's digging my gear and he ain't about to tell me. That's just how some brothers are.

"Who?" I ask. I only got one boy and I was hoping he wasn't talking about Bone.

"Bone. He ain't tell you?" Phil says looking at me as if he is shocked that I don't know.

"Naw, man. That's business. He ain't got no reason to share that with me." Bone fat tail is ridiculous. He knows good and well this bamma is not to be trusted. Bone will mess with anybody to keep them Benz car payments up. He can be so stupid sometime.

"Oh, alright. Well, if you talk to him before me tell him I should have something for him in a couple of days. Tell him I said to call me."

"Alright, I'll let him know." I say and start walking. I had to split. Tyanne is probably fuming since she hasn't heard from me to wish her Happy Valentine's Day.

"Oh, I heard that group Jodeci is supposed to be at Champions in a few weeks. Is that a rumor or what?" Phil asks as he walks to catch up with me.

"Naw, man. It ain't no rumor. I'm trying to work it out, but it's rough. Here it is February and they're already booked out through the summer. But I'm working on it."

"Let me know if you need me to step in," He says, "My cousin is going out with one of them so I can get you hooked up if things don't come together. Let me give you my number." As he writes his number on a piece of paper, Pancake Butt joins us and is staring me all in my face. She really needs to stop playing because I ain't even a little bit interested.

Dudes trip me out trying to act like they got all kinds of connections. Even if he could get me a hook up with Jodeci, I wouldn't be looking to him for help. Not only is he not to be trusted, he talks too much. I can see him now going around telling everybody if it wasn't for him I wouldn't have ever been able to get Jodeci to come to Champions. Naw, that's okay buddy. I take his number anyway to make him feel good.

"Yeah, just holler at me and let me know. I can get you hooked up." He says and leans in for a brother arm grip. "Oh, and don't forget to tell Bone to get with me."

"Alright, man." I say, peep at my watch and jog to the car. Man, I can't wait to talk to Bone so I can cuss him out for being so stupid. The reason he didn't tell me he is messing with Phil is because he knows I would be the first to tell him how dumb he is.

Later for this. I gotta get home to my baby. She's

probably still mad at me for not going to church with her this morning. When I say no to the little Sunday morning church invite, that usually sets the mood to bad for the rest of the week. I really don't see how she expects me to get up for church service on Sunday morning when I don't get home until three or four o'clock in the morning from Champions. No way am I going to anybody's church after having just a couple hours of sleep.

This is the thing. Tyanne thinks that everybody is supposed to jump and do everything she says because some voice told her it was time for her to get her life together or whatever it was that happened when she gave her life to Christ. I don't know what it was, but whatever it was, our thang ain't been the same since.

It was right after them bammas came up in my apartment and stole my money. That whole thing messed Tyanne up real bad. It seemed like forever that I watched Tyanne walk around the house crying and yelling at everybody. She was acting crazy as a junebug. I just made sure I stayed out of her way because there were times when I just wanted to body slam that girl. It wasn't until her Aunt Ruby started taking her to church that she started to get some focus and started acting jive like the Tyanne I remembered. A little on the strange side, but she did calm down.

There was that one church service I'll never forget. It was the Sunday we both went to church, right after the robbery. The preacher talked about reaping your sow or reaping what you sow. Something like that. I was jive tired but I remember him talking about everything we do in life will catch up with us eventually. Whether good or bad, whatever we put into life is what we get out of life. He also talked about not waiting until we're old and gray to begin a relationship with Jesus Christ.

I watched Tyanne the whole time. She was really tuning into this dude. Before I knew it, her and some of the chicks and even some of the brothers walked up to the front of the church. Some of them were crying. Some of them just stood there with their hands in the air. Tyanne fell to the ground with her hands raised and was crying as hard as I don't know what. I was jive concerned because I had never seen Tyanne that way. I think she was the loudest one in the church. As I was on my way to pick her up, one of the ushers put her white gloved hand up in my face and told me to leave her alone. She told me that Tyanne was being delivered. In my mind I'm thinking, delivered where?

After the service was over and we were riding home, I asked her what was going on with her when she walked to the front of the church. She said she decided to give her life to Jesus Christ and wanted to change her ways and start living right. I didn't quite understand what all of that meant, but I decided to leave it at that.

Well, little did I know that was the beginning of a new and different Tyanne. Before that day, she was fun, outgoing and had a bit of adventure in her. But after that walk up to the front of the church that day, she changed a lot.

For the first few months, she started going to church non-stop. Not just on Sundays, but two and three days through the week. She started cutting back all her girlfriends and would just hang out with them old ladies from church. She even started talking old, saying stuff like, "God is good all the time and all the time God is good." Everything was God this, God that. I mean I respect God, but come on man. Tyanne was taking this holy stuff too far.

Eventually she stopped wearing the clothes I bought her. She said they were "whorish." She didn't want to wear anything tight. Clubbing was out. Eventually she stopped coming into Champions. She said she didn't like the atmosphere. She just became a whole different person. She started nagging me every Sunday morning about me not going to church and told me that I was going to hell if I didn't accept Jesus Christ. I hated when she said that to me. I believe in God. I'm just not into that whole church thing.

Not only that, I don't have to go to church every Sunday and give the preacher all my money to go to heaven. I have a problem with people giving all of their money away to the church anyway. All the preachers do is ride around in big Lincolns and Mercedes while everybody else in the congregation need their cars fixed. Don't get me started with the whole church thing.

Bottom line, it just got bad between me and Tyanne. She wasn't hearing me. And I sure enough wasn't trying to hear her. I was at the point where I was seriously thinking about leaving Tyanne. She wasn't the woman I married. Then I thought about my kids. I love my kids and the last thing I want to do is leave my family the way my father left us. So instead of leaving, I went to the one person that could get to Tyanne like no one else - her Aunt Ruby. I explained to Aunt Ruby that I didn't mind that Tyanne was going to church but she had become hell to live with. I asked her to please talk to her niece and let her know that she was driving me up a wall and she was running me away.

Well, after Tyanne and Aunt Ruby had the talk, I noticed things slowly began to change. Tyanne wasn't pressuring me as much about going to church. Her attitude wasn't as bitter and nasty and she even loosened up a little more in the bedroom. I'm thinking, what all did Aunt Ruby say? Go head Aunt Ruby with your bad self. I just know we started communicating more and overall things changed for the better.

Although, things are a lot better, she's still not the Tyanne I married. Not that we have a bad marriage, we just don't see eye to eye on some things. I tell Tyanne that this is my life. Just because she done seen the light or whatever, don't mean everybody else is going to burn in hell. Tyanne has changed a lot, but I'm dealing with it, because I love her. But she's been making it real rough lately. If I can just get her to put on these thongs tonight, I believe we can work it out.

CHAPTER THREE
Tyanne

Patrice catches up with me after church service and invites me and the kids over for what she jokingly refers to as "tea and crumpets." Her husband Melvin has an emergency trustee meeting immediately following church with Pastor so Patrice and Melvin won't be celebrating Valentine's until later in the evening. Marcus usually spends Sunday afternoon playing basketball or organizing things over at Champions. I don't expect him to be home any time soon so I take Patrice up on her offer.

The tea and crumpets turn out to be macaroni cheese, baked teriyaki chicken, collards and strawberry lemonade. As usual, the kids make their plates and go to the basement to watch a movie. I sit down at the island in the kitchen as Patrice washes dishes.

"How do those greens taste?" Patrice asks.

"Pretty good," I say with my mouth full. Patrice knows she can cook like a country woman. She is always fishing for compliments when it comes to her food.

"I thought they were going to be too salty because the top fell off of the shaker when I was adding the salt and… "

"Nope, they're just right and you know it Patrice."

"I don't know it," Patrice says trying to hold in her laugh. "That's why I asked."

"Yea okay," I say sarcastically and shake my head.

"Girl, did I tell you that I was doing Ms. Gertrude's hair yesterday and she asked me if I was pregnant?"

I nearly choke on my food from laughing. Patrice laughs out, too. Not as though it weren't a possibility as Patrice is still in her childbearing years. It's just that we were just talking about her recent weight gain and how she's planning to get back into the gym.

"That's not funny Patrice." I say, trying to regain my composure. I love that my friend can laugh at herself and not take life too serious.

"Go ahead and laugh. You know what I told her?" Patrice says with her lips turned up as she does when somebody gets on her nerves.

"Oh my goodness, Patrice, what did you tell her?"

"I said real serious like, you know what? I might be Ms. Gertrude, but I'm not sure. I'll let you know when I find out though."

"No, you didn't lie to that woman like that?"

"What? Was I supposed to say, no I'm just fat as a buffalo? Besides, you know Ms. Gertrude is nosier than a private eye investigator. I love her with the love of God, but she is a nosy woman."

"Girl, you are a mess."

"Speaking of a mess, when are you coming to the salon to get your hair done? It's been in that tired ponytail for way too long. What's going on with you?"

"To be honest, I haven't been thinking about my hair." I take a sip of lemonade as I think of good place to begin sharing my heart.

"I know that's right, but the ponytail is not working. Those brittle ends make me nauseous every time I look at them."

"Please. I'm just trying to figure out the right words to say to Marcus tonight when I tell him I'm leaving him."

Patrice stares at me in silence with her hands on her hips as suds run down her legs. "Girl, don't play with me. Are you serious?" She asks with a look in her eyes that waits for a punch line and at the same time holds out for hope.

"I'm very serious. I'm through."

"Don't be through. God's got it." Patrice says and turns back to the dishes.

"Maybe He does, but my mind's made up."

"Oh really? What about the mind of God?"

I don't answer. Knowing well aware that God is not the author of confusion, my head starts to spin any way. My mind can think of many reasons why I should leave Marcus, yet my heart and spirit never match up with any of them.

"Ok. Don't answer." Patrice says. "I'm just going to pray for you and Marcus. All that other stuff that you are about to come up with is probably irrelevant anyway."

"Well, thanks Sister Patrice for the encouragement. I feel so much better."

"Chile,' I'm not even here to make you feel better. I'm here to provide tea and crumpets and to tell it like it is."

I pick up my fork, pretend to throw it at Patrice, but instead shake my head at my no nonsense friend. She was never one to accept more than a millisecond of murmuring and complaining. I've come to her on many days with a hundred reasons why I believed I needed to leave Marcus and each time she would redirect my focus on having faith in God. Yet this time, I'm not looking for direction. My mind is made up.

"Well, I plan to have one last talk with him tonight." I say. "Depending on how it goes will determine whether or not I pack up this weekend."

"And if and when you pack, where are you going?"

"I haven't figured that part out yet. I guess to Aunt Ruby's or maybe a hotel. I don't know. All I know is that something has to change."

"And you think you and four kids in a hotel room is the change you need?"

"Patrice, I'm serious."

"So am I. I just think you're growing frustrated with some things and now you're taking your focus off of God."

"Yes, you're right. I'm very frustrated. I'm also more focused than I've ever been in my life. There is so much that God is requiring of me and I believe that in order to get where He really wants me, I must make some changes in my life. Pastor's sermon today confirmed that for me."

"Okay, that's all well and good Tyanne, but remember this scripture, too, 'beware lest somehow this liberty of yours become a stumbling block to those who are weak.'"

"I hear you."

"You don't have to hear me. Hear God."

Before I can respond, the kids come upstairs and request some of Patrice's delicious homemade apple pie and French vanilla ice cream. We follow them down the basement with our bowls filled to the rim with pie and ice cream and watch the movie, "Sister Act." Well, at least everyone else is watching it. My mind is locked on Patrice's 'Hear God' comment.

"Speculative."
"S-p-a-c-u-l-a-t-i-v-e"

The kids and I get home at around six o'clock that evening. I'm sitting on the couch helping Summer with her spelling words when Marcus walks in the house carrying a long box and a Victoria Secret's bag in one hand, scooping Jordan up with the other.

"No, Summer. There's only one "a" in speculative. Try spelling it again." I walk to the kitchen, open the refrigerator and look for nothing in particular. I just don't want to look in Marcus' face. If there is no eye contact, I can keep the attitude going. Something about that man makes me melt and lose all equilibrium whenever I look at him.

"Daddy!" Summer yells with excitement as she runs and climbs all over Marcus. Every time Marcus comes home it's like he has just returned from overseas or something. I see it as an indication of how much he stays in the streets. Marcus just basks in it like he's Father of the Year.

"Hey, Princess," Marcus says carrying both Jordan and Summer as he follows me into the kitchen. I grab an apple and cut them into slices for Jordan. I feel Marcus staring a hole through my back. I'm determined not to give him one ounce of attention.

"Daddy, are you still coming to the spelling bee next week?" Summer asks.

"What day is it?" Marcus asks despite the fact that Summer has told him a billion times already.

"I told you it was next Thursday, Daddy." Summer reminds him as she wraps her arms around her Daddy's waist and looks up at him as if he can do no wrong. That's when I turn around and look him right in the eye. I wait for him to make up an excuse as to why he can't make it. I'm ready to jump into his stuff. Marcus is famous for conveniently forgetting when he doesn't want to do something.

"Yea, baby. Daddy will be there." He says, cocks his head and licks his tongue playfully at me. Marcus thinks he can fix everything with humor. Usually he can, but not tonight.

"Yes!" Summer says as she does her little happy dance around the kitchen floor.

"Alright, Summer. Time to get back to those spelling words," I say.

"And how are you doing, sexy legs?" Marcus asks smiling at me as he walks to the stove, lifts the pot cover and begins inhaling the sweet, zesty aroma of my world-famous spaghetti.

"I'm fine. Bone called." I say without looking at him and place the sliced apples in front of Jordan.

"Alright, cool," Marcus says and hands me the Victoria's Secret bag and a box. "Happy Valentine's Day. I love you baby." He says and kisses me softly on the cheek. "I'll be upstairs waiting for you."

This is just like Marcus to buy me something to try and make up with me. I wait until I hear the shower cut on in our room, before I sit at the table and look at his so-called love offering – a teddy and some thongs. Real cute, but he won't see it on me tonight. I open the box and inside there are a dozen yellow roses. I inhale the sweet scent and tears fill my eyes. Marcus knows how much I love yellow roses. This brings back memories of the time he picked some from this lady's yard years ago to give to me and her Doberman pincher almost bit his hand off. We laughed about that forever.

I read the note card through teary eyes:
Let's make love ~ M
Until now, I didn't believe it possible to love and hate a

person at the same time. Part of me wants to put on the thongs and throw Marcus on the bed and let him know how much I love him and want us to work out while the rest of me wants to run upstairs and throw the whole pot of spaghetti in the shower. I feel so many different things, but most of all, I'm angry. I cried past hurt a long time ago. Anger and bitterness are now tearing away at the core of my heart. And there is no way that a teddy, thongs and a dozen yellow roses are going to change the way I have been feeling.

After I finish cooking dinner, give Jordan his bath and finish up with Summer and her spelling quiz, it's already after ten. Tiffany went to bed earlier than usual and Lil' Markie, Jr. is in his room playing with his Sony Playstation when I walk up the stairs.

"Alright, Markie. Time to put the game away and take your shower." I say.

"Aw come on, Mom. Just a few more minutes?" Lil' Markie whines as he nearly stares a hole in his TV and punches the buttons of the game control.

"Right now Marcus." I say firmly and stand in the doorway until he shuts the game down. I quickly survey the state of his room. Dirty clothes and socks are strewn about while the hamper sits empty. "And do something about this room before you get in the bed. Thank you very much."

When I walk into our bedroom, Aaron Hall's "Let's Chill" is playing low on the radio as Marcus lays in the bed with his legs crossed and nothing on but his briefs talking on the telephone. No matter how angry I am at Marcus, just looking at him turns me on. I want to jump on top of him and kiss him all over. Marcus has that sexy Michael Jordan thing going on – tall, bald and handsome as he wants to be. Even so, with every ounce of strength within me, I fight off the strong desire to look at his chock full of honey, smooth and sleek body. Marcus manages to keep his youthful figure without doing any exercise. A genetic gift as Marcus likes to tell me when he's full of himself.

From the way he's talking, I can tell that it's Bone on

the phone. "Yeah, man. I'll just page you in the morning and you let me know then. Alright, later." He says and hangs up the telephone. It never fails. All telephone conversations with Bone cease whenever I enter the room.

"Hey babe." He says as he runs his hand in a circular motion across his chest. His introduction to foreplay, I suppose. I pretend not to notice.

I walk past him and throw the bag with the teddy and thongs on the dresser. Making sure I am in his full view, I step out of my dress baring all my goodies in a pair of black bikinis and matching strapless bra. Freeing "the girls" from the strapless bra, I throw on a big tee-shirt and then prance into the bathroom to take out my contact lenses. I can feel Marcus staring at me like a panting puppy, but he can pant until his tongue falls out for all I care.

"What's wrong with you?" He asks as if he really doesn't have a clue.

"Nothing's wrong with me. I guess I'm just wondering why every time I come in the room and you're talking to Bone, you hang up the telephone."

"What? When did it become a crime for a man to have a private conversation?"

"Won't you stop trying to be so slick and admit that you are still in the game Marcus?"

"Still in the game? Where did that come from?"

"Yeah, okay. Play dumb." I climb into my side of the bed, pull up the covers and curl up away from him.

"Look, Tyanne. I told you I wasn't selling no more. Why would I lie about that?"

"Then why is it you're still dealing with Bone, the biggest hustler in DC?" I yell as I pop up out of bed like a jack-in-the-box.

"What? How do you sound? Me and Bone been friends way before I started hustling. What? I'm supposed to stop being his friend because you don't like him?"

I can tell he's getting angry. He starts rolling back and forth in the bed tugging at the covers. "Girl, you need to stop trying to control everybody. That's my boy and he gonna be my boy whether you like it or not."

"Marcus, I know you like a book and you need to stop faking. There's something you're hiding and you know it."

That's when it gets strangely quiet.

"Look, Tyanne," he says as his tone softens a bit and he sits up in bed, "I've always told you the truth. I'm not in the game anymore. I'm not selling. Bone just wants me to drop something off for him. I'm making me a quick thousand and that's it."

"Drop something off? Marcus, that's just as bad." All I can do is shake my head. It's obvious the spirit of deceit and corruption has reared its ugly head in our home once again.

"Tyanne, I know what I'm doing, okay?"

"No, it's not okay, Marcus. You really need to step out of that fantasy world you're in. Do you even consider that you have a family? Obviously not. And this whole thing with Champions. You're not really serious about running a legitimate business, are you Marcus? That's just a cover up."

"A cover up?"

"Yes, a cover up!" I literally feel my blood pressure rise as my forehead begins to thump. "Stop using Champions as an excuse to run the streets Marcus. It's played out!"

"Oh, here we go again with this bull. Tyanne, shut up, will you? Because you don't know what you're talking about, just shut up."

I take a deep breath and will myself to remain calm and not burst into tears. I hate when he disrespects me this way. I want to lash back at him, tell him to shut up, kiss my butt and anything else I can think of, but I made a vow to God after our last argument that whenever Marcus spoke to me like this I would not go tit for tat with him. If I did, we'd be at it all night. Instead, I ignore his remarks and choose my words carefully so that he hears what's really on my heart.

"Whether you have noticed it or not, I've had it. I've had it with you, Champions, all of it. I'm tired of you staying out all night, the women calling here and pretending its business, you coming and going like you're some bachelor and I'm your maid. You don't even notice that I'm sad and depressed, because all you can think about is Champions. Marcus, I never see you. The kids never see you. We need you Marcus!"

By this time, tears are flowing, spit is flying and my arms are flinging – I'm out of control. I so desperately want to talk this out sensibly, but my emotions have taken over. I realize it's already a lost cause, but I walk to the door anyway and close it shut to try and stifle the noise so the kids won't hear. Especially Jordan. A few weeks ago when Marcus and I were arguing, Jordan ran out of the house crying. Marcus is able to stretch his voice to an octave that is inhumane. It even scares me sometimes.

"I'm working Tyanne! What do you want me to do? Huh? I can't be in two places at one time. It's a business. A business can't run itself."

"I understand that." I say and lower my tone, hoping he will follow suit. "I just feel that we're growing apart. It's like we don't even know each other anymore. We don't do anything together. We don't talk. You don't even ask me about what's going on in my life. I don't even think you care."

"What about you? You spend all week in church. When do I ever see you? Don't try and make it all about me. Ever since you got saved, I don't know who I'm dealing with from one day to the next. Let you tell it, everything I do is going to send me straight to hell. I can't win with you."

Okay. I know that I can be super spiritual sometimes. But still.

"Oh, Marcus, it's deeper than that and you know it. Alright. Let's take Champions for instance. When we started Champions, we were a team, right? We decided everything together, right?"

He just raises his eyebrows and waits for me to finish.

"Well, lately it's just been 'I'll choose the groups' and 'Tyanne, you do the paperwork.' You don't even keep me in the loop anymore. I overhear most of what's going on with Champions by overhearing your telephone conversations with Bone."

"Stop faking. You don't really care what's going on with Champions. You want to be as far away from the club as you can. Isn't that why you decided to do the paperwork from home? So you wouldn't have to be in that *atmosphere* as you call it?"

"Look, I just feel that since I'm supposedly managing Champions that I should have some say in what groups we book. You knock everything I suggest. For example, like the gospel group suggestion I made... "

"Okay, so this is what this is really about? Gospel groups?"

"Hear me out Marcus! I made the suggestion that we book gospel groups or some jazz groups. Change the flavor a little bit. Get some Kirk Franklin, Hezekiah Walker, Fred Hammond, groups like that. You and I both know that DC always packs out gospel concerts. But every time I bring it up, you knock it."

"Yeah, well that's not my crowd. People know Champions for its R&B & go-go flavor. Not gospel and jazz. That's a whole other venue that I know nothing about."

"But I do. And besides, you can learn about it. Gospel and jazz music is booming. And if you're worried about the money, don't. If you line up some well-known names and good local talent, people will come out. You would be surprised at how God would bless you financially if you pull in some gospel groups. Not only that, God can get the glory at the same time."

"Nah, God can get His glory another kind of way. That ain't me." He says, shakes his head back and forth like a little kid. He picks up the remote and starts changing channels again.

"Ok. Well, if it's not you. Let it be all me. Let me handle everything." I ask feeling my stomach sink as I watch Marcus push the buttons on the remote – an obvious sign that my time is up and he's beginning to tune me out.

"That's alright," He says shaking his head no. "That ain't me. I'm not trying to bring gospel groups to Champions."

"Why does it have to be about you all the time? This is something I would like to do so that I can feel as if I'm a part of Champions. There's nothing you would have to do. Please? At least give it a try."

"Look, you have to spend money to make money. And if we go and put up the money and don't make it back, we lose. Point blank. I'm not trying to lose money while you try and prove a point."

"You won't lose any money. Not with the names I'm going to line up. Just give it a chance, Marcus!" I feel myself losing control. I can't help it.

"Tyanne, I don't want to bring gospel into Champions, alright? Everything is fine, just the way it is. Nothing's broke, nothing to fix. So can we change the subject, please?"

Marcus is so stubborn sometimes it makes me want to beat him silly. He turns the channel to an old black and white movie. At this point, I know for sure he is just changing the channels to be changing them because he hates black and white movies.

I sit back on the bed, cup my face in my hands and then I say what I've wanted to say for so long. "Well, I think you better start looking for another manager, because Champions ain't me no more." I didn't want it to come out like that. Yes, I did. I said it the way I meant it. I've had it.

"So what are you saying? You're not going to manage Champions anymore?"

I hate when he rephrases what I say and makes me answer the question directly with a yes or no, because usually after I give a yes or a no that's the end of the conversation and he goes into his evil silent treatment.

"Marcus, what I'm saying is that I think you should give my idea a chance. Let me prove to you that it will work."

"No. You just told me that I better start looking for another manager. Are you no longer managing Champions? Answer the question?" He's hurt. I can tell the way he's breathing.

"I just think you're being stubborn and selfish and there

are things I see us doing together instead of apart. That's all."

"Are you or are you not going to manage Champions? Just answer the question Tyanne!" He demands as loud as he can without popping a blood vessel.

Be strong and of good courage Tyanne. Stop being a punk and say what you mean. "No. I'm not." I answer knowing we've now arrived at the end of our conversation. So I beat him to it. I turn off the lamp on my side and pull the covers up on me.

"Yea, okay." He says as he clears his throat and swallows hard as he does whenever he's angry and is trying to calculate his next move. "When's your last day?" He asks as he turns his body away from me and starts to brutally pull on the covers. Marcus knows he has enough cover.

I don't answer. Emotionally I had stopped managing Champions a long time ago.

"Yeah, okay. Cool. Just get all the books together before you go to work in the morning and leave everything on the desk at the office." He says calmly, but in a wicked kind of way. He then turns off his lamplight, props his head up on his hand and stares at the television. I know he's not watching it because that old black and white movie is still on the screen.

I pull the covers up as far as I can without suffocating myself. I didn't want Marcus to hear me cry. Though I would give any and everything for him to grab me, tell me he loves me and that he'll do anything he has to not to lose me – but I know that isn't going to happen. As always, Marcus will hear my cry of hurt, pain and frustration and pretend not to hear. He eventually flips from the black and white movie to Russell Simmons's Def Comedy Jam on HBO. Here it is my heart is broken and he chooses to fill the room with jokes. I cry myself to sleep as I know moving day is only six days away.

CHAPTER FOUR
Marcus

If it wasn't for the juicy kisses Jordan, Lil Markie and Summer hit me with between the eye and nose, I could have slept another twenty four hours. An argument with Tyanne always leaves me more tired than a twelve round bout with George Foreman.

"Have a good day, Dad." Lil' Markie yells. Jordan copies him as they jog down the stairs. Jordan thinks his big brother is the stuff. If Lil Markie gets a haircut, he wants one. If Lil' Markie gets a pair of new sneakers, he wants a new pair. I get a kick out of watching the way Jordan looks up to his big brother and how Lil' Markie looks after him. I would have loved to have had a brother growing up. Instead, I had my big head sister Pam bossing me around all the time. I love her though.

"Don't forget my spelling bee on Thursday." Summer reminds me and runs after her brothers.

"Alright, alright," I say and cover my eyes from the sunlight coming through the blinds. Normally Tyanne wakes me up before heading out to work with a kiss or a to-do reminder or something. All she left this morning was the scent of her perfume. No kisses, no touchy feely, no nothing.

"Daddy, can I have some lunch money?" Tiffany asks, holding the jeans I had on the night before in her hands as she does every morning before school. "Hurry up. Ma is waiting in the car."

"Yea, alright girl, calm down."

As I dig into my jeans pocket for my wallet, I check out Tiffany's outfit. Sometimes she can go overboard showing too much of her shape, but today is cool. She has on a pair of jeans with a Washington Bullets sports jersey and a tee-shirt underneath. I hand her five dollars.

"Thanks Daddy." She says, kisses my cheek and runs down the stairs just as Tyanne blows the horn. I walk to the window and watch them pull out of the driveway. Then I think about last night.

Tyanne is tripping.

For real.

At first it was all about me coming out the game and doing something legal, now I'm off the streets and she still talking trash. Tyanne and the kids have never wanted for anything. I've always made sure they had a roof over their heads, clothes and plenty to eat. I wanted my kids to have what I didn't have which was a father that loved them, was there for them, bought them what they needed - just straight up being a part of their lives.

Shoot, I've had my run in the hustler life. I'm just trying to make me a quick few dollars, that's all. I'm through with the game. After all my boys started getting locked up and brothers started getting killed over territory, I pulled out. I was scared straight. Then I had to deal with not knowing what else to do when I decided to stop hustling drugs. All I had ever known was the streets. I just barely finished high school. I never went to college and being a part of corporate America never did turn me on. The last thing I wanted to do was put on a tight suit and go faking with them corporate bammas. My sister Pam was forever calling my mother crying every other day about how she felt her boss was racist and is trying to stop her from being promoted. And how all the white people seemed to get promoted over the black people. And that you have to act a certain way to get into certain groups or cliques. Who wants deal with all that bull?

I decided I wasn't going through all of that just to make a dollar. I would make my own money and be my own boss. I had made all of my money back from the robbery and I was ready to do something legit. That's when me and Tyanne sat down and had a long talk about me coming off the streets. She was happy as I don't know what. She came up with about a billion ideas. She even tried to talk me into opening up a daycare, but that wasn't me. If I was going to do something, I wanted to be able to feel it and enjoy it. I don't want to do something just to be doing it.

Anyway, my boy Bone told me about the sale of the building that used to be Fancie's Nightclub. He said the owner was looking to sell it for little or nothing because he was moving down to North Carolina. The property could sell for over $150,000 easily but the owner would settle for $50,000 cash, no questions asked. Good gugga mooga. That was a steal.

What I did was tap into what I had saved up, hired a few contractors and had the building completely renovated. Three floors with chandeliers, marble floors, state of the art big screen TV's, full bars on each floor and the baddest sound system on the East Coast. No doubt Champions laid all the other clubs in the area to rest. We had a big grand opening night with some local football and basketball players and yelled it out over all the local radio stations. Yeah. It took off like lightening. I don't know if people were just looking for some place new to party or if the timing was just right. I don't know what it was, all I know is that I made my fifty thousand back in the first year and then some. I think that's jive alright for a young boy who didn't finish high school.

It's a good feeling to be able to make your own piece of money on the legit. My mother always told me that I got my street hustler attitude from my father. All I can do is take her word for it. I barely even remember too much about the brother. The one memory that stands out in my mind is when he took me to the carnival. I believe I was about six years old. He bought me all the hot dogs, soda and cotton candy my stomach could hold. And I remember this woman that was with him that was all over him. He kept telling me to call her Aunt Dee. I might have been six, but I had sense enough to know that Aunt Dee had no business kissing on my father. I made sure my mother found out about it when we got home. Man, I started something bad by running my mouth. My mother went off. She started crying and yelling and throwing dishes. They ended up fighting. It was real bad.

The police came, but by the time they got there, my father had left. And that was the last time I saw the dude. A family destroyed all over some woman he probably cared nothing about. After that, I promised myself I would never, ever let another woman come between me and Tyanne.

    Let me get up and get my day started. I talked to Bone last night and he told me he could hook me up with his cousin Mocha and she would help me out around the office. I just need her to do a little paperwork over the next few days. While Tyanne is acting simple and tripping, I got a business to run. Hopefully by the end of the week she will be over her monthly tantrum and back to her old self.

    After I put a few coats of wax on my cherry-colored, 928 Porsche that is guaranteed to make heads spin, I take a shower; throw on a fresh navy blue Fila sweat suit and a spanking brand new pair of black, Stan Smith Adidas. I jump on the beltway and blast Guy's album:

    Groove me!
    Baby!
    Tonight!

    Yeah! Teddy Riley and Aaron Hall don't have to ever in life make another album after this one right here. Every cut on this album is banging. Come to think of it, I should try and get them to come to Champions this summer. Oh, yeah, that would be a sell out for real! Maybe I'll talk to this Mocha chick and have her set it up for me.

    I pull off the beltway and take the scenic route to Bone's house straight down Georgia Avenue into Northwest. The city is in rare Monday morning form. Howard University students make their way from their dorms to the campus through smells of oils, incense, fried subs and French fries while junkies and drunks take their spots on the corners and porch stoops; sounds of Africa and R&B boom from the speakers posted at door entrances and drown out my music as Asians and Muslims sweep the entrances of their storefront spaces. DC is fresh and alive like this every morning and I love every minute of it.

    The plan is to pick up Bone so we can go meet his

cousin Mocha for lunch and discuss her helping out at Champions. When I pull up in front of Bone's house blasting Slick Rick's "Hey, Young World," his grandfather is sitting on the porch sucking his gums and watching people and cars pass by.

"Hey Pops, what's happening?" I say as I climb the steps and open the screen door with no screen in it. That door has been like that forever. Pops just kind of nods his head. He never says much.

No matter what time I walk into Bone's house, Dionne, who has been Bones' girlfriend since like the third grade, is always frying something in the kitchen. This time it smells like fried fish. Yep. Fried fish it is. Bone's big tail is sitting on the couch, wearing what looks like a size 10X dingy tee-shirt and a pair of elephant size boxers as he wolfs down a platter of fish, fries and a liter of some off brand coca cola.

"What's up player?" Bone says with ketchup on his shirt looking like a big chocolate hippopotamus, never taking his eyes away from the TV. He's watching the soap opera, The Young and the Restless. He can tell you everything going on with Ms. Chancellor, but can't seem to get his own life together.

"Man, I thought you were going to be ready?" I ask irritated with a crinkled forehead to match. Bone is trifling when it comes to being on time.

"I am ready." He says as he finishes his last bite and starts to laugh. I don't see anything funny.

"Why are you eating knowing we're about to have lunch?"

"Let me worry about my stomach and you worry about yours. I'm about to go in this bathroom and make some room for lunch anyway. Alright buddy?" Bone laughs as he wobbles to the back of the house.

"How you doing Dionne?" I ask trying to be polite. Dionne can't stand me. Every since elementary school when I threw a snowball and hit her in the face and knocked off her thick eyeglasses. Can't a sister forgive?

"How you doing Marcus?" Dionne answers without

looking up from her plate. I know she really doesn't care how I'm doing, she was just being nice. And I'm sure she thinks she looks like a million bucks with her pink Gator shirt, some too small shorts showing all of those chittlin' things on her thighs, baby powder on her neck with lint in her finger waves. As long as Bone loves her I guess that's all that matters.

I don't know why I am trusting Bone to hook me up with someone in his family to help me with Champions anyway. I have to trust that Bone knows how important this is and that I need somebody to help who has some sense and knows what they're doing. He told me that Mocha has been here for a few weeks and has been interviewing trying to get a job as an attorney. I guess if she's smart enough to get a law degree, she has to have a little sense.

Downtown DC is crowded with no parking as usual. Me and Bone sit double parked outside the court building in Bone's green 190 Mercedes waiting for Mocha. When she walks to the car, my mouth hangs open so wide a hundred flies could have flown into it. Now to see Bone you would think everybody in his family looks like Herman the monster. But baby is sexy. A little on the tall side, she has that Tyra Banks thing going on with a honey blonde bob and a tan form fitting suit that shows off that big, round butt. As she approaches the car, she looks past me, smiles at Bone and climbs into the back seat.

"Girl, what took you so long?" Bone teases her.

"Shut up, Christopher," she says giggling and then looks at me. "He's so rude. Hi, I'm Mocha." She says and reaches to shake my hand.

"Hi, Mocha. I'm Marcus." I say, returning a firm handshake as I top it off with a LL Cool J licking of the lips.

"I'm starving Christopher. Where are we going to eat?" Mocha yells over Chubb Rock's, "Treat 'Em Right" blasting from Bone's new car speakers that he is obviously pressed to show off. I turn it down so I won't have to deal with Bone's yelling and spitting over the music.

"We ain't going no where if you keep calling me Christopher." Bone says. "What you got a taste for?" Bone asks looking at Mocha through the rear view mirror. "Pizza? Italian? Or that grass food you be eating? Marcus, she be eating alfalfa sandwiches man."

"Don't knock it until you've tried it!" Mocha says as she playfully taps Bone on the back of his head. "Take me to Georgia Brown's. I hear they have some good food."

"Yeah, Christopher, take us to Georgia Brown's" I tease Bone trying to get in on the conversation.

"Oh, he's been like that about his name ever since we were little. He always said his name sounded like a white boy's name. I try to tell him there's a lot of power in his name. A name like Christopher James Reynolds can open a lot of doors. My name, well, people know what color I am right off the bat."

"What, you don't like your name?" I ask.

"Yes, I love my name. It's just that there's no guessing my race when you're checking out my resume' that's all."

"Well, if they call you they obviously know they're getting a Black sister named Mocha. So they must be interested right?" I ask smiling.

"I guess you're right." She laughs and leans back in the seat. I steal a peek at her through the passenger side mirror. Baby is *real* sexy.

Since it's the lunch rush, Georgia Brown's is a little crowded. But with me and Bone knowing nearly everybody in the DC Metro area and being regulars, we manage to get a seat in minutes. Mocha orders a salad, I order some crab cakes and Bone orders the catfish with shrimp and grits. As we wait for our food, Mocha and Bone catch up on family happenings and then the conversation turns to Champions. Finally.

"So, you fired your wife Marcus?" Mocha asks looking at me with a half smile.

"What?" I look at Bone wondering what he's told Mocha about me and Tyanne.

"Girl, I didn't tell you he fired his wife! What's wrong with you?" Bone says as he laughs nervously and has that familiar embarrassed look on his face. I can tell he's been running his mouth. That's all he does.

"Oh, I'm just kidding," Mocha says and grabs her salad and lemonade from the waiter. "Bone, told me what happened. Actually, it was the other way around, right?"

Bone runs his mouth entirely too much. "I guess you can say that." I say, take a swallow of my iced tea and then stare at sexy trying to figure out her angle. Was she going to help out or not? That's all I wanted to know. Tyanne picked the wrong time to act stupid. Hopefully Tyanne will be back to her old self soon, because this one here is full of jokes. I'm not on joke time. Not today. "So, you're pretty good with administrative stuff?" I ask trying to get her off joke time and focused on Champions.

"Yes, I like to say I am. What kind of business software you working with on your computer?"

"Oh, baby, you going to have to ask my wife. I couldn't tell you."

"Alright, no problem. We'll have your wife fill me in." Mocha says.

"So can you start tomorrow?"

"Whoa!" Mocha laughs out. "Bone was serious when he said you needed somebody fast."

"I told you that Mocha," Bone says and wolfs down his food as if somebody is trying to take it from him, "This dude right here is a straight up business man."

"Baby, look, I got a business to run. I'm looking for somebody who is serious and ready to work. And the money I'm going to pay you might even make you rethink your little attorney job."

"Oh, really? So you're going to pay me a hundred and fifty dollars an hour? Well, you're right. I might just rethink this little attorney job."

"Attorneys make a hundred fifty an hour?" I ask. Bone lets out a quick laugh to remind me of how much I don't know.

"Uh- huh," Mocha says. "And some make much more than that."

"Alright, well I'm not going there, but I'll make it well worth your time. For now, I just need you for a few hours a couple days this week to type up some contracts and make a few phones calls. Finish eating. I'll swing you over there so you can see the club. You can meet Tyanne and she can get you familiar with everything."

"Yeah, ok. Ya'll go rolling up in there thinking Tyanne is Ms. Nice Church Girl if you want. Don't get my cousin beat up man." Bone says laughing and coughing at the same time with food falling out of his mouth.

"Aw, go 'head man, it ain't even like that and you know it." I say handing him a napkin to clean up. If I hadn't, he would have just kept right on eating with food all over his face.

"Now, don't tell me she's one of those ghetto bunnies waiting to go off on me?" Mocha asks.

"Naw, baby. It ain't like that. My wife is a very respectful woman. Don't listen to Bone."

"Alright, I'll take your word for it." Mocha says as she finishes the last of her salad and then excuses herself to the ladies room. I watch her until she is on the other side of the bathroom door.

I have to stop looking. Baby is doing something to me.

CHAPTER FIVE
Tyanne

Someone asked a question
Why do we sing?
When we lift our hands to Jesus
What do we really mean?

No matter how many gospel songs I listen to in the car on the way to work, the argument Marcus and I had the night before keeps swirling around in my head and takes my thoughts elsewhere. I drop the kids off to school and call my supervisor, Darnell and tell him I'll be late for work. As much as I want to just dump any and everything that has to do with Champions, I have to drop by the office to finish up some paperwork and close out this big contract for Marcus. As fed up with him as I am, my heart won't let me leave unfinished business hanging like that. Besides, I know it means a lot to Marcus to have PLC (Players and Lovers Chillin') perform at Champions.

Aside from Guy and Jodeci, PLC is quickly becoming one of the hottest groups in R&B. Marcus wants to book them for a Spring Bling party at Champions. Not only does he want to book them, he wants me to be the one to talk the price down with their manager, Dukey Wills. Dukey manages a lot of the new young R&B groups, so whenever you want a hot group, more likely than not, you have to deal with The Duke.

As I hold the line and wait for Dukey to come to the telephone, I see Marcus and some chick walk through the office door. He's got to be kidding. She and Marcus walk past me as if I'm not sitting there. He shows her around the office and then takes her out to the party area. A surge of anger hits me so hard I accidentally drop the phone. I would have hung up the telephone if I hadn't heard Dukey say hello.

"Oh..uh..hello, Dukey. This is Tyanne. How's it going?"

"Can't complain. What's cooking, good looking?"

"You and PLC."

"Oh, they bad, ain't they baby? You like the skinny one, don't you? Look a little bit like Marcus, don't he?"

"No, I don't like the skinny one and no he doesn't look like Marcus." Dukey is used to me laughing and joking with him - not today, not with Marcus and some little valley girl walking around here pretending like I'm invisible.

"Yes, he does. You just don't want to admit it because you think I'm going to tell Marcus on you. I won't tell, baby. If you are digging on a young boy, that's alright. This is between me and you." Dukey says and bursts into hearty laughter and then starts coughing from years of cigarette smoking. Dukey is his usual self and I am not in the mood.

"What you asking for PLC?" I ask.

"Oh, you want to go straight business with me today, huh? Well, since I'm in love with you, we can go five thousand."

"Come on, Dukey. This is Tyanne. You can do better than that."

"I'll tell you what. If you get me a date with your little sister, we can go forty-five."

"We go four and it's a deal."

"You got it."

"Ok, deal. Four it is." My sister, Janelle would kill me if she knew I used her name to close a deal with Dukey.

"Alright, so what's her number?"

"I'll have her call you."

"She better call me, too. If not, the next time I'm going to treat you like an enemy. You don't want that trouble from The Duke baby."

"Yea, okay."

"I'm serious."

"Ok. Fax me the papers Dukey."

"Alright, baby. I'm here when you get tired of Marcus."

"Goodbye Dukey."

"Alright, baby."

Dukey is one of a kind. You have to play his game every time. He needs a woman bad. I wasn't about to get Janelle involved with his nasty butt. She already has enough problems chasing after that no good, womanizing boyfriend of hers. No need in a bringing her another bag of mess. Especially Dukey Wills who has to be the biggest freak in the music industry. Although my sister would probably love to play him for his money and I on the other hand would love to see her with anybody other than the conniver she's with now. My sister's love life is another story for another time.

This would be the ideal time to let Marcus know that he is able to get PLC for a thousand dollars less than he had anticipated, yet it seems he's tied up with his little lady friend. I'm not going to hang around and be disrespected. Just as I am about to grab my purse and car keys, Marcus and Barbie or whatever her name is walk back into the office.

"Mocha, this is my wife Tyanne. Tyanne, Mocha. Mocha is going to be our new manager."

Manager? Oh, really? Okay, he's trying to be cute. I'll play along. I'm not about to let him get me all riled up. Not in front of Barbie.

"Hello, Mocha." I say and shake her hand as tight as I can without breaking her fingers.

"Nice to meet you," She says with her little valley girl accent.

"Oh, by the way, Dukey agreed to four." I say to Marcus, "He's faxing the contract. Just sign it and get it back to him." I gather my things and head for the door.

"Yeah, boy. Alright, that'll work." Marcus rubs his hands together with over the top excitement. "Uh, Tyanne, don't leave yet. I need you to show Mocha what you do on a day-to-day basis. Get her familiar with the computer program, the contracts and things like that. I'm going to run to the bank. I'll be back in about a half hour." Marcus pats his pants pockets for his keys and jogs out. If he could have done a 100-yard dash he would have but that would make it too obvious that he's avoiding any response from me.

"Marcus, I have to…" I start to tell him I have to be at work, but he has already bumped past me and is out of the door.

Marcus is really showing his butt. He actually brings in some young girl to manage the business we built together with sweat, fears and tears? It'll be a cold day in you know where before I sit down and teach some little overdone Barbie doll the family business. I'm not sure what kind of game Marcus is playing, but my patience is quickly growing thin.

"Marcus showed me around. This is a really nice club. I've seen some of the clubs in the area, but yours is really upscale compared to the rest."

"How do you know Marcus?" Forget the chitchat.

"Oh, I know Marcus through my cousin Bone. Actually, I just moved out here from Philly a few weeks ago and have been looking for a job in my field. I'm an attorney." She says and pauses as if she's expecting me to salute her on being an attorney. I just look at her to finish. "So when Bone called me this morning and told me that Marcus needed some help with the club, I was like, heck yeah. I could use the extra money. And any friend of Bone's is a friend of mine."

Oh, my goodness. Thoughts of tackling her to the ground overtake me. *Lord, please rid me of these evil and wayward thoughts.* "Look, honey. I'm not sure what Marcus explained to you about your reason for being here, but… "

"Well, the way I understood it…" She cuts me off which makes me all the angrier. "… is that you weren't going to be helping anymore and he needed someone to manage the office?"

One… two… three. *Breathe Tyanne.* "First, let me make this clear sweetheart. I'm not the help, ok?" I say as my hands find their way to my hips and my head tilts to one side. "Seems you've gotten yourself in the middle of something that is far beyond your understanding and I don't believe you want to be in the middle of this."

"Look, I just came to help Marcus out." She holds her palms up in defense, "I'm not here to get in the middle of a marriage squabble,"

"There's no marriage squabble. Just a little misunderstanding, that's all."

"Hmph. Seems to be more than a misunderstanding to me. Marcus has a need and you can't seem to satisfy it."

For a second, I feel my head turn all the way around like Linda Blair in the Exorcist movie, but I know that can't be because I'm saved and filled with the Holy Ghost. *Breathe Tyanne*. This young girl is trying me sure enough.

"Excuse me?" I give her a chance to rephrase her statement. I stand with my arms folded as I know that tucked away is the best place for my hands at the moment.

"Woman to woman?" She continues, "You have a very, handsome and sexy husband. Do what you need to do to satisfy him, because there are others who would be more than happy to."

"What's your name? Mickey? Mocha?"

"It's *Mo-kuh*."

"Mocha, I don't need you giving me advice concerning my husband, okay?"

"I'm just trying to help you hold on to that scrumptious man of yours, that's all. We had lunch earlier and he was panting for me like a puppy in heat. If I really wanted to, I could have served him a little bit for lunch."

"I'm going to ask you to leave before I say or do something I'll regret." I say breathing heavily with a thumping headache from holding in more than a mouth full of ungodly things I want to say.

"Oh really?"

"Yes. Really," I say and take a step toward her. *Lord, have mercy.*

"Actually, I'll need to wait for Marcus. He's supposed to take me home."

"You can wait for him outside, because you're not staying in here." I place my keys and pocketbook down on the desk and unfold my arms. She took me there.

"Yea, let me leave, *Minister*. We wouldn't want you to lose your religion, huh? Hmph, you church ladies trip me out." She says as she pulls her pocketbook strap over her shoulder and walks to the door. "Tell Marcus I look forward to seeing him later."

Only the strength and power of God kept me from knocking her upside her head. After the door closes behind her, the tears that were burning my eyes fall, but the anger I feel won't allow me to break down. Just as quickly as the tears fall, I wipe them away. I'm so angry I can barely see straight. Marcus has some nerve bringing that girl in here. It just shows that he could care less about me, my feelings or our marriage.

I start not to even go to work, but I know the job is what I need to keep my mind busy until rehearsal later. Before I leave for work, I call Patrice and tell her everything.

"Tell me you're lying?" Patrice says. I can hear her licking her fingers, probably cake batter. When she's not at the hair salon, you can find her somewhere baking something. Any other day I can tolerate the licking and smacking, but today it is incredibly annoying.

"I wish I were."

"I still say, trust God."

"Trust Him to do what Patrice? And can you stop smacking in my ear?"

"Oh, I'm sorry about that." Patrice laughs her goofy laugh. "But anyway, trust Him to do whatever He wants to do."

"I'm tired. Really, I am. I can't do it anymore."

"Well, if you want the truth, you're the one who opened the door for the enemy to walk in."

"What are you talking about?"

"Tyanne, once you declared in your heart that you were done trying and that you were leaving Marcus, the enemy got busy. The devil is just doing what he does best. You? You're confused, back and forth and the enemy is having a field day. The word of God says that a double minded man is unstable in all his ways. You don't know what you want from one minute to the next Tyanne. You either want your marriage or you don't."

"I'm married to the mob Patrice!"

"Ha! I'm glad you can find humor in all of this. That's why I love you. But all jokes aside. Do you or do you not want your marriage?"

"Yes… no… not like this. Yes, I want my marriage, but not like this."

"Ok, so make up your mind what it is you want. God is not the author of confusion. And you're a confused mess right now. Tell God what you want and then go take it back from that 'ole slew footed devil. All God wants from you is to be the wife He called you to be. He is faithful that promised. Just trust and believe that He's going to work it out."

Patrice was right and I knew it. I hadn't been where I was supposed to be spiritually in a while. I hadn't been praying as I should, my thoughts had been devilish and Lord knows I needed to repent for my thoughts concerning that Mocha chick.

I sigh heavily. Patrice has known me long enough to know my sigh means that I am tired of it all and I need her to intercede for me.

"Come on. Let's pray."

Patrice prays for the up building of my faith, against my defiance and my nasty attitude.

That's why I love Patrice. She never hesitates to call me out when I'm wrong. She has never been afraid to hurt my feelings, especially if it means saving my soul.

Patrice and I have been friends forever. As God would have it, Patrice and I lived right next door to one another growing up. My mom, little brother and my sister and I stayed with Aunt Ruby and her kids. I think I was about nine years old when my mother who was a heavy drinker and big on parties, left for the West coast with her junkie boyfriend. I haven't seen or spoken to her since. My father – well he's been locked up in jail ever since I was a toddler. That left my super-religious, chain-smoking Aunt Ruby to raise me and my siblings. The rule was we could only go as far as the front porch when we played outside. Ms. Wanda, who was Patrice's mom, applied the same rule to Patrice. So that's where our friendship started – on the front porch.

Growing up, Patrice and I were so close people would often mistake us for sisters. As far as we were concerned, we *were* sisters. When we were in about the fifth grade, we poked our pointer fingers with needles and pressed them together and declared from that moment on that we were forever "blood sisters."

Because we lived so close to one another, there was barely a day that would go by that we weren't together. And we did everything together. And I mean *everything*. From stealing Barbie dolls from the corner store when we went to get cigarettes for Aunt Ruby to losing our virginity to a set of twins with big afros in our first year of high school. As Aunt Ruby would say, we were just two little "grown" girls who were well beyond our years and needed our tails whipped.

We were always the first girls on our block to try something new. And we always did it together. We were the first on the block to get perms – right on the porch. The first to get our ears pierced – on the porch. And we were the first to go out with the coolest dudes in the Northeast area - Marcus and Melvin. Patrice and I met them during a high school basketball game. They had to be the flyest dudes that we had ever seen. Two young dudes fortunate enough to have their own cars in high school while the rest of us were either walking or catching the bus. You couldn't tell me and Patrice nothing when they pulled up with their shiny Nissan Maxima's. Marcus had a black one. Melvin's was white. They never needed to blow their horns or get out of their cars. They would always pull up bumper to bumper with their radios blasting. The bass would make the front room walls thump, which would always cause my Aunt Ruby to start yelling at me.

That was our cue. I would call Patrice so that we could make our grand exits out the front door together. By the time we opened our doors and started down the porch steps, the whole block was either on their porches or peeping through the curtains. Patrice and I were the feature attraction on many nights.

Marcus and Melvin made us into two wannabe fashion models. They bought Patrice and me any and every little thing our hearts desired. Soon the whispering started that Marcus and Melvin were making their money illegally. You think we cared? As young and stupid as we were, we just kept spending and pretending to be the models that never made it out of the hood. All that mattered was that we had on a different outfit everyday and a hair appointment every Friday. All we knew were parties, restaurants, and concerts. Any place we could go to show off an outfit and a hairdo. Not that I should boast, but we looked good. At sixteen, we had the bodies of twenty-five year olds. We looked so good we had both men *and* women pausing whenever we walked by. We had become two hood bunnies who had become real comfortable with just walking around spending money and looking cute.

That lasted about two years until Melvin got busted and we were jolted back into reality. Melvin did about two years, got saved in jail and came home and got a job with a courier company. Patrice started working as a secretary with the government thanks to her sister. Both Melvin and Patrice started going to church and kept their distance from me and Marcus, but I couldn't blame them. Marcus wasn't in any hurry to pull out from the game.

As for me, I ended up getting pregnant and Marcus had a fit. He tried everything to keep me from having Tiffany. He yelled, cried and screamed about how we were too young to have kids and that we couldn't afford to raise a child. Whatever. There was no way I was going through with another abortion. I had already had one and it was devastating to say the least. The secret I tried to keep from Aunt Ruby was uncovered after I started hemorrhaging so bad that I almost had to have a blood transfusion. No way was I putting my body through that again. Besides, I wanted our baby.

Aunt Ruby was past hot. She said if I wanted to act like I was grown then she was going to treat me like I was grown. Aunt Ruby gave me one month to get a job and find my own place. That kind of pressure will make you grow up real fast. In retrospect, I thank God for Aunt Ruby making me step up and deal with my responsibilities. Eventually I got a job and Marcus and I got an apartment and "played house" as Aunt Ruby called it. And then to add to the stress, Aunt Ruby started getting on me about "living in sin." She made it clear time and time again as to what the Bible said about a man and woman living together unmarried. She reminded me that it was "better to marry than to burn."

At the time, I was no churchgoer nor was I a Bible reader, so I took Aunt Ruby's word for it. Lord knows I didn't want to burn in hell for my sin. As a result I gave Marcus an ultimatum: marry me or I'm leaving. He told me he wasn't ready. I left with Tiffany on my hip and our clothes stuffed in trash bags. Two days later, Marcus came and proposed to me.

Whatever happened to that kind of love? The kind of love where he believed I was worth it? From what I saw today, I meant no more to Marcus than some New Jack Swing club manager. *God, unless You work a miracle, I'm outta here this weekend. I can't do it anymore.*

CHAPTER SIX
Marcus

Something ain't right. When I get back to Champions, both Tyanne and Mocha are gone. I call Tyanne at work and she tells me she put Mocha out. Put her out? I try to get more information out of Tyanne as to what happened, but she says she's busy at work and she can't talk. I page Mocha about a hundred times, but she has yet to call me back. I call Bone and ask him has he talked to Mocha. He says no and asks can I drive him somewhere because his car is in the shop.

"I need you to take me to one more spot." Bone says as he gets back in the car.

"Man, this ain't no limo service."

"Aw, stop crying." He says and hands me the money he promised.

"Where you wanna go?" I ask.

I don't know what possesses me to ride with Bone to do a drop off deep in the hood of Southeast. Everybody knows this area is hot with drugs and cops and is not the place for anybody to just be parked sitting in a beaming 928 Porsche. In a split second a few stick up boys can pull up on you with a gun, take your money, your drugs and your ride or the police can pop up and do a random, strip search. I guess I'm just not thinking. Bone practically begged me to drive him. Plus he peeled me off a couple of hundred bucks for the ride and I ain't never turned down the opportunity to put a few dollars in my pocket.

Bone directs me to pull up in front of one of the apartment buildings, gets out and walks up to a girl standing out front wearing a hot pink ski vest and matching Timberlands boots. She has her back turned, but I can't stop thinking that her shape looks real familiar.

What the? I know Bone don't have the nerve to have

his arms wrapped around that pancake butt chick I saw in Victoria's Secret with Phil Perry? Bone puts some money in her hand, kisses her and gets back in the car smiling like he just hit the jackpot or something.

"Bone, what are you doing man?"

"What?" He has the nerve to try and look clueless.

"You messing with *her*?" I ask and nod at pancake butt who is counting the money as she walks back into the apartment building.

"Who Nicole? Naw, not like that."

"Then like what? That's Phil's girl, man."

"I know that. I was seeing Nicole long before Phil even came into the picture. Me and shortie go way back. Stop tripping man."

"No, you stop tripping. You that pressed for some booty? I just saw her and Phil together the other day. So she playing both of ya'll, huh?

"Naw, she ain't playing me 'cause I know about Phil. Besides, man I'm not trying to marry the girl. You know what I'm in it for player, right?" Bone laughs and put his hand up to give me five. I leave him hanging. I wasn't giving him five on that mess. Bone ain't got a little bit of sense.

"She's a freak man and she's not to be trusted." I say, "You need to use your brain instead of that piece between your legs. For real man."

"Yeah, whatever. I know you ain't talking. And just because you and Tyanne in a war and she ain't giving you none don't be trying to block mine." Bone turns up the volume on the CD in the car and sings along with Frankie Beverly's "Golden Time of Day" trying to irritate me.

"You still haven't heard from Mocha?" I ask and turn the volume down.

"Naw, she haven't called me yet. And man, you knew good and well Tyanne wasn't having all that with you and Mocha."

"Having what?"

"Oh, you thought you were just going to bring Mocha in there like that and everything was going to run smooth as silk?"

"Bone, look man, if Tyanne not trying to have nothing to do with Champions, then why she gonna act simple when I get some help? I got a business to run. She needs to grow up."

"Look at who you brought in to help? You don't bring in nobody that look like Mocha, what's wrong with you? You supposed to get somebody about five hundred pounds that got a face like a moose." Bone busts out laughing. He's right. Mocha is sexy and phat to death. I just hoped Tyanne hadn't said anything to her to the point where she isn't going to help out.

"Hey! Stop right here!" Bone yells. "I want to go in this carry out so I can get me a sandwich. I ain't ate since earlier today."

"What? You just ate. You must have a hole in your stomach or something."

"Man, look I'm just built differently than you. I gotta keep my energy up."

"Well, I'm not going to help you to your grave and take you to that grease hut. That's a suicide stop right there. Ride with me to my Mom's house. She'll hook you up."

"Oh, ok, that works. Miss Tilda knows how to hook a brother up."

Yeah. I've been missing my moms anyway. And she is crazy about Bone. Other than Melvin, when we used to hang out, Bone is about the only dude I can bring into my mother's house without her making little sly remarks. She never did trust too many of my friends. Moms be having a third eye when it comes to my friends. And when it's all said and done, the ones she don't trust end up being the cruddy ones.

When we pull up, I can see straight through the window from the outside. Mom is standing in the kitchen running her mouth and hot pressing somebody's hair.

"Ma, it's me!" I yell as I unlock the door. "I got Bone with me."

"Come on back. I'm in the kitchen."

The house is filled with both cigarette and burnt hair

smoke. As usual, the TV is blasting in the living room with nobody watching it. I turn it off and take a quick peek at the mail to see if there are any letters from my buddies in jail. There's nothing but a few sweepstake letters and some bills.

"Hey Ma" I kiss her cheek and taste that nasty, powdery make up she always puts on.

"Hey, Miss Tilda," Bone says and goes up and gives Ma a hug.

"Hey, baby," Mom says as she twists her lips away, blows out her cigarette smoke and smashes out what is nearly a whole cigarette in the ashtray. She knows I hate to see her smoke.

"Can't you speak?" Mom asks as she pokes me with her elbow, "You remember Pat, Ms. Jackie's daughter?"

What? This was Pat? Back in the day, Pat was one of them skinny church girls who couldn't come outside. Pat done filled out real nice. She look's a little like Sheneneh from *Martin* in the face, but still.

"How you doing?" I ask as I grab two bottled waters from the fridge, throw one at Bone and try hard not to look at all those curves.

"I'm fine." She says and gives me that little look that tells me she's digging me. I look away. Although Tyanne's been withholding her goodies from me, I'm not about to get into any trouble with Pat. It's not worth it.

"What brings you by here?" My mother asks as she runs the hot comb through Pat's hair and blows onto her scalp.

"To see you. And Bone was hungry." I say and look inside the refrigerator.

"Now, why you blaming it on me, man?" Bone yells from the couch.

"Aw, go ahead with that shy stuff boy." My mother yells back at Bone. "You know you can come over anytime for Miss Tilda's good cooking." My mother washes her hands and pulls plates from the cabinet. She always has to take over the kitchen "Get out of my way boy." She bumps me with her hip. "How's your mother doing Bone?"

52

"She's back in the hospital, but she alright."

"What? She got that fluid on her lungs again?"

"Yes, ma'am" Bone says as he walks into the kitchen to watch my mother heat up a few pieces of fried chicken and puts them between two pieces of Wonder bread. She hands Bones his sandwich along with a bottle of hot sauce and a side of baked beans.

"Tell her she better stay on top of it. My brother... Marcus, you know your Uncle Al? He dealt with that same thing a few years ago. Nearly took him to his grave. Tell her to leave that cheap beer alone. They say that cheap beer got a tendency to build up in your lungs. And that sauerkraut, too. I know your mother love herself some sauerkraut. I do, too. But she gotta leave that sauerkraut alone. "

"Yea, I know. I'll tell her." Bone so fake. He wasn't gonna tell her nothing. He was just being polite because he was eating.

"Oh, lawd, we got Doctor Tilda in the house ya'll." I joke and pour me and Bone some Hi-C orange drink.

"Marcus shut up before I scalp you with this hot comb." My mother says. "You know your momma know what she talking about. Neither you or your sister barely ever had to go to the doctor when ya'll was growing up because Doctor Tilda knew how to take care of you the old fashioned way."

"Alright now!" Bone says and bites into his chicken sandwich.

"How's little Jordan?" Pat asks as she stands and stretches all those curves. Got to be more careful! Baby is stacked and she knows it. She reaches into her pocket and gives my Moms twenty dollars. It's good to see Moms done stopped doing hair for free.

"Oh, he's doing alright." I say.

"I remember the last time I got my hair done. He was here talking up a storm."

"Yeah, he loves to talk. He got that from his grandmother." I look at my mother and smile. I can see her gray hair coming in more through her short cropped afro. It looks good against her caramel complexion. Mom has never been one to try and wash away the gray. She'll tell you that she "earned her gray" in a heartbeat.

"I also heard on the radio that your wife is going to be singing in a concert with jazz artist Nile Rivers on Wednesday." Pat says. "You must be proud of her, huh?"

"Yea. I am."

"So what's this about Tyanne singing in a concert? Ain't nobody told me about a concert." My mother says standing with her hands on her hips.

"Ma, I did tell you about it." I say licking my fingers. I can't remember if I told her or not. I've been so busy at Champions I may have forgotten to tell her. Besides, my mother never has been into a whole lot of Gospel stuff anyway.

"Boy, if you told me I wouldn't be standing here looking crazy."

"That's right, Ms. Tilda." Bone says, "He always trying to act like he told somebody something. He does me like that, too."

I shake my head at Bone. He can act real simple when his stomach is good and full.

"Ms. Tilda, I'm surprised you haven't heard about it." Pat says, "It's been on all the radio stations. I even saw a short commercial on TV. My girlfriend went and got us tickets and said they were just about out of tickets."

"Since when you need a ticket to get into church?" My mother asks looking perturbed. Mom was never a church fan and I believe some of her anti-church beliefs have rubbed off on me.

"No, it's a free concert. You just need a ticket to get in. I believe they are just trying to keep count of the crowd." Pat answers.

"So, Marcus, man did you get me and your Mom's a ticket to the concert or what?" Bone teases as he rinses his plate in the sink.

"Ma, you know I got you a ticket." I didn't, but I knew I could get them from Tyanne. Shoot, let my Moms show up without a ticket and not be able to get in. I'll give that church the blues.

"How are you getting to the concert Ms. Tilda? You can ride with me and my girlfriend if you want." Pat asks.

"Oh, okay baby. I appreciate that. I may try and make it if I don't have to go to my Elk's meeting. What time does it start?" Ma asks looking at me. I take a bite of my sandwich and feel guilty because I'm not up on it.

"Seven o'clock" Pat answers. Good thing she does, because I have no idea. I really should know more about this concert, but Tyanne has been in a real nasty mood lately and we haven't been able to say two words to each other without arguing.

After Pat leaves, me and Bone hang around and talk to Ma for a little while. We talk about how she feels I don't bring the kids around enough and that I don't visit enough since we moved to the suburbs. We talk about how all of her renting neighbors are losing their homes from the owners selling out. It's a sellers market in DC and owners are taking advantage of sales in the high numbers. I didn't realize that my mother was about the only one in the neighborhood who actually owned and wasn't renting. My mother has always been smart when it comes to handling money and investment matters. I guess that's where I get my business savvy. From there, her and Bone start talking about the soap operas and that's when I know it's time to go.

I drop Bone off to pick up his car from the shop and he follows me over to Champions so we can get ready for the "Hood Auditions," a little something I thought of to give peeps in the neighborhood an opportunity to showcase their talent on stage. You never know, I could be the next Berry Gordy discovering talent right in my backyard. I hold it once a month and each time the line ends up wrapped around the building. This evening is no different.

As I pull into my reserved parking space with the sign posted in front that says, "HNIC," my pager goes off. I look at the number. It's Mocha.

Finally.

I walk up to the club, say my hellos to all the honeys

and the fellas, give dap to the staff and go into the office and call Mocha back.

"Hey Marcus," Mocha answers on the first ring.

"Hey, what's up? What happened earlier?" I ask.

"I don't think your wife is too happy with me helping out. She put me out."

"She did what?"

"Yeah. She thinks I want you. I can understand her feeling that way with you looking like Denzel and all. I explained to her that I have a man and it ain't like that."

"I can't believe she tripped out like that." I say and pretend not to hear the part about Denzel. Shortie is good for my ego.

"That's alright. I just wanted you to know that I am still willing to help out. Just tell me what needs to be done and I'll figure it out and get it done. I'll use my computer to do it if we have to. I just believe in what you're doing Marcus and I want to do all I can to help."

"Thanks Mocha. I appreciate that."

"Just call me when you want to go over everything."

"Alright, thanks."

Now that's what I'm talking about. Mocha is willing to look past Tyanne's foolishness and still help a brother out. I can't wait to get home to give Tyanne a piece of my mind about how simple she's acting.

It wasn't until I received my routine after-school page from the kids that I realized I hadn't talked to Tyanne all afternoon. I was used to her paging me at least twice by now. I'll give it to her though; she's doing a good job of playing hard this time. But that's alright, two can play that game.

I check the books to see who is scheduled to work the restaurant. With The Hood Auditions going down, the crowd will reach the maximum for sure. I'll need full staff working tonight. These young boys I hired to work the evening shift have a habit of calling in or coming in late. When I came up off the streets, I pulled a lot of the youngins from around the way and gave them jobs at Champions. It was my way of helping to keep them out of jail and a few dollars in their pockets. We all know the money don't pay as much as they can get paid slinging drugs, but at least it's legal money.

"Marcus Miller?" Standing in my office doorway is a young dude with a huge gold chain, a white tee, jeans and a black leather jacket. His face isn't familiar but I am sure he is about to break out into a rap or a break dance. He just has that look about him.

"Main man, the line is outside." I say.

"Oh, my name is Andre. I hope you don't mind me coming back here, but one of the waiters told me I could come on back."

"Naw, that's cool. What's up?" It's not cool for real. Dude could be coming back here to rob me. These young bammas on security don't know anything about looking out for nobody. I'll have to holler at them later about just letting people come back to the office without checking with me first.

"I just wanted to drop off this cassette for you to listen to. My group is on there – One Love. We're a new up and coming R&B group. We're just trying to get out there and hoping that we could do an opener here one night. If you just listen to it man, I'm sure you'll dig it. It's three of us. People say we remind them of Bel Biv Devoe."

"Oh, okay cool my man." I say. "You got a number?"

"Oh, yeah" He hands me his business card.

"Alright. I'll listen to it and if it's good, I'll get with you."

"Thanks man. I appreciate it."

I close the door behind him and stick the tape in my cabinet drawer. As soon as he said they were like Bel Biv Devoe that messed it for me. Up and coming artists need to spend more time on being original rather than trying to be like another group. Youngin needs to know that Bel Biv Devoe is in a class all by themselves.

That girl is poison! Poison! Poison! Poisin! Poisin! Ha! That's the joint right there!

Speaking of Bel Biv Devoe, Tyanne is supposed to see if she can get them to come to Champions this summer.

There is a lot I need to speak with Tyanne about concerning the club. She sure picked the wrong time to start acting up.

I call the house to check on the kids. Summer answers the telephone.

"Hi Daddy."

"Hey baby. Everything alright? Where's everybody?"

"Tiffany's not here. Just me and Markie. Oh Dad? I got a B on my math test, but I got an A on my spelling test!"

"Now, that's my girl. I'm proud of you baby. Keep up the good work, ok? Let me speak to Lil' Markie."

"Oh, I forgot to tell you. Markie he… "

"Give me the phone girl!" I hear Lil' Markie yell and then the phone drops. Summer is hollering through the phone trying to tell me something that Lil' Markie doesn't want me to hear.

"Hello? What's going on?"

"Hey Dad. Everything's alright" It's Lil' Markie.

"Did you do your homework?"

"I'm doing it now Dad."

"Alright. I'll see ya'll later tonight."

"Alright."

I start to call Tyanne with her so called busy self, but decide to leave it alone. No need in getting myself all worked up. Besides I need to get out front and get the auditions started.

As always, Bone and this jive time local music producer named Sean Cooper help me with the judging. A little bit of everything is lined up; lots of SWV and Mary J. Blige wannabes, some Keith Sweat and R. Kelley look-a-likes and all the New Edition, Guy and En Vogue sounding groups you ever did want to hear. Most of them sound alright, but midway through the auditions, this older dude comes through, and for a minute makes us forget where we are.

With his white suit set off with a lime green shirt, matching white hat and white shoes, he hands the DJ his cassette, puts his information sheet on the table and steps to the microphone to sing his version of "Jesus Is Love" by Lionel Ritchie. He quiets the whole room with his vocals.

There is something about this dude's voice that makes me feel like God has just walked in the building. Usually, me or Sean would cut the singer or group off after the first few minutes, but neither one of us had the nerve to cut this dude off. This brother sounds good. For a split second, I'm thinking it's a set-up and that he's somebody that Tyanne sent. But the more I watch him I can tell this brother is on his own and in his own little world. Besides I didn't want to think Tyanne knew anybody who would wear a white suit, white hat *and* white shoes.

After he's done, I nod at him and tell him we'll be in touch. Instead of heading for the door, the dude with the white suit comes over to where I'm sitting.

"So what you think?" He asks.

"Oh, you sound real good man." I say. "We have a lot of good acts coming through here. If we can get you in, we'll be in touch."

"You think my head screw on and off, don't you buddy?" He says as he leans in closer to me.

"Huh?" Dude catches me off guard. He looks at me with a weird grin spreading across his face.

"You know you ain't about to let me get up there and sing that song at your club, are you young man?"

"Look, pops," I say and shake my head for Bone and the other two security dudes to back up. Obviously they're preparing for whatever was about to go down. "You sound good and all, but you know what we got going on here. This is an R&B crowd."

"Yeah, I know what you got going on here. You got a whole bunch of sin going on here, that's what you got. You need to let Jesus up in here boy. All this boom boom music and drinking and carrying on, you need to wake up my brother. Our time here on earth is short, you better be trying to let God into your heart before it's too late."

"Alright main man. You can start heading for the door now," Bone says and steps closer to him. Although white suit had put a halt to what we were doing, I wasn't trying to hurt or disrespect him. I figure if you just let him talk, eventually he'll chill and move on. At least that's what I was hoping.

"Oh, what you gonna do? Bum rush me big boy?" White suit says to Bone. "You better sit your tail down somewhere boy. I ain't afraid of you. I came in here with Jesus and I'm leaving with Him. If you knew what I knew, all ya'll would get with Jesus. Life is too short." He says, tilts his white hat and walks toward the door.

"Have a good day Grady." Sean says and the crowd busts out laughing. I assume Sean is talking about Grady from Sanford & Son. I wasn't about to laugh. Yeah, white suit was a little irritating, but I wasn't about to laugh at the man of God.

The whole thing strikes me as kind of strange though. Especially since it's the last thing me and Tyanne were arguing about last night. Ain't nobody ever came through this line auditioning a gospel song. Now, out of the blue, pops wants to turn Champions into a church service. I'm gonna have to ask Tyanne about that white suit.

The next dude up made all of us quickly forget about white suit. This dude looks like Babyface Edmonds in the face, has the wavy hair like him, talks like him, but I be dag on if he sounds like him. Aw man. He gives the DJ the music for, "This Is for The Cool in You" by Babyface. As soon as he sings the first line, "Here we go round and round and back and forth" and starts to do the rock, I know it's gonna be a long night.

CHAPTER SEVEN
Tyanne

Tuesday, February 16

Four o'clock in the morning. That's what time Mr. Marcus rolls in. And he has the nerve to curl up behind me when he gets into bed. I lay as still as rock. If he wants some, he had better go on back to where he came from because he sure isn't getting any of this.

When the alarm goes off at six, I pop up like a flap jack, but Marcus doesn't budge. It must have been some night at Champions. Although I don't smell liquor on him, I know he's been doing something he has no business. I try hard not to let my imagination get the best of me, but come on. A night club with scantily clad women and he comes in at four in the morning - give me a break.

I drop the kids off at school and then I do the one thing that always makes me feel better: I cry all the way to work. I play my favorite Yolanda Adams CD and get it all out. I arrive at the office with the saggiest face and blood shot eyes ever. I walk past Darnell's office and I don't even say good morning. I can't. I don't want him to see that my eyes are blood shot red from crying. But of course, he has to come and get him a full eye view of me anyway.

"Were you able to get in touch with Jeffrey Beacon on yesterday?" Darnell asks and peeks into my office.

"Yes, I did as a matter of fact," I say as I shut on my PC and pull my coffee mug from my drawer without looking directly at him. "Jeffrey says that tomorrow at two o'clock is fine." I hand him two completed reports. I know Darnell is grateful to have me as his administrative assistant. Not only am I efficient and most professional, Darnell can trust me.

The sister I replaced just a year ago had embezzled thousands of dollars from him. He asked a mutual friend at church if he knew of any trustworthy administrative assistants who knew accounting, and lo and behold I was recommended.

"Everything okay?" Darnell asks with a look of concern. He's used to me cracking a joke on him. I couldn't even conjure up a knock-knock joke if somebody had paid me. Darnell had no idea of the trouble I'd seen in the past twenty four hours.

"I'm fine. What about you?"

"You know me. I'm a soldier." Darnell says, "By the way, what are you doing for lunch today?"

Now, where did that come from? The devil is always busy. Darnell has never invited me to lunch before. I'd always assumed he had respected the fact that I was a married, church going woman who would never entertain the idea of going to lunch with her married, adulterous boss. It's obvious he's totally disregarding the brown paper bag lying on my desk.

"Thanks, but no thanks. I brought my lunch." I say and drop my eyes to the brown bag just in case he missed it.

"Oh, yeah, you did." He says trying to look all innocent. "What about tomorrow?"

"What?" I don't mean for it to come out that way, but Darnell is really throwing me for a loop with this one. Does he realize that I am the same woman who takes all of his messages from the billion women that call the office looking for him?

"I *asked* what about tomorrow?" I can tell by his facial expression that this moment is getting uncomfortable for him.

"Probably not," I say as politely as I can, "Actually, no. We can't go out to lunch."

"Mmm. I see." He says as he plays with his moustache. "May I ask why not?"

"Darnell? What in the world is going on with you?" I almost laugh.

"There's nothing wrong with me." He says looking embarrassed, borderline irritated. "I just wanted to take you out for lunch to cheer you up. If you don't wanna go, that's cool. It's just that you come in here and don't even speak and then you tell me that everything is fine. I know you're lying."

"I'm fine really. Nothing God can't handle. I appreciate your concern though."

"So no lunch date, huh?" Darnell says and forces a huge smile to mask his obvious embarrassment as he backs up in the direction of his office.

"Darnell, go get some work done, *please*." I say half smiling and dismiss him by looking down at my work.

"Oh, by the way, I'm looking forward to the concert tomorrow night." I hear him say as his office door closes.

All I can do is giggle to myself. The attention is a bit flattering, but I know better than to even daydream about Darnell. He's a big bag of sin walking. The one I feel sorry for is his wife. I met her for the first time at our Christmas party last year. She looked real sad to me. She spent most of the evening forcing laughter and conversation, but I know pain when I see it. I see my face in the mirror every day, so I recognize it. It was obvious by her extra weight that she was trying to eat her pain away. Darnell probably never takes her anywhere and all she does is stay in the house and take care of their kids while he runs the streets. Ha! Whose life does that sound like?

Every time I think about Marcus, I feel I'd be better off by myself. I mean he loves me and I love him, but what happens when love isn't enough? I just feel so lonely. Even when he's in the house, I feel lonely. We try to talk, but I know he's not interested in what's going on with me at church. He could care less. And he lets me know when he's not interested when he starts turning the channels with the remote while I'm talking. I want a man who adores me and respects my spiritual relationship. Marcus is completely turned off by it and to be honest, I'm at the point where I'm completely turned off by him.

The tears are starting again. Just as I get up to close my door and give into a good wailing, the phone rings and reminds me that I am at work and not at the church altar. I pull myself together.

"Darnell Martin and Associates?"

"Well hello there Mrs. Miller."

It's Nile. I take a deep breath to ward off the crying spell. Lately, all it took for me to cry was a soft voice or for somebody to bump into me hard enough.

"Hey, Nile. How are you?"

"I can't complain." He says with the bass of James Earl Jones. "Hey, I'm calling to confirm tonight's rehearsal. We still on?"

Was he kidding or what? Seven o'clock can't get here soon enough. "Oh, yes. I wouldn't miss it for the world."

"Good. We're going to finish up the last few tracks. If we stay focused, we should be able to have everything wrapped up tonight. Oh, and we're not meeting at the church tonight, we're meeting at the studio. And you know the area is pretty live, so call me when you pull up so I can come down and walk you up."

"Alright, sure will. Seven o'clock right?"

"Yes ma'am."

"Okay, I'll be there."

"Thanks Tyanne."

"Okay, bye."

Feeling my mood change immediately from distraught to hopeful, I sit back in my chair and think about the CD, the release party and how God is blessing me to finally move forward with my dream. At that moment, the troubles between Marcus and I, Mocha, Champions and anything that is not related to the upcoming concert on Wednesday seems insignificant. I am determined to remain steadfast and immovable and allow God to use me in a mighty way. If God be for me, who or what can be against me?

* * *

After picking up Jordan from day care, my intention was to go straight to my bedroom and lay down a moment before starting dinner, but not before I walk in the house and deal with Lil' Markie who I find sitting on the couch holding a plastic bag of ice on the side of his forehead.

"What happened to you?" I ask. Summer starts laughing. I don't see the humor in it at all. After I shoot her a look, she drops her smirk and looks back at her textbook.

"I was fighting. But it wasn't even my fault." Lil' Markie pouts and hands me a piece of paper. It was a letter from school stating that he was being suspended for three days for fighting another student.

"Look, slow down and tell me exactly what happened."

"Alright, me and Troy were going to seventh period and these two dudes came walking behind us talking about they gonna take our sneakers after school. So we kept on walking and... "

"Do you know these two guys?"

"Yeah, I've seen them around. I don't really know them, but anyway, we kept walking and then one of them came up to me and said 'What you say young boy?' and he grabbed my collar like this." Lil' Markie pulls on my collar for emphasis. He's always so dramatic when he tells his stories with his pint-sized self. Apparently his attempt at trying to win me over so he won't get himself grounded.

"So I pushed him off and then he swung at me and we just started fighting. So Mr. Talbert came out after all the kids started gathering around and making noise and everything and then he took us in the office and we got suspended."

See, this is what I'm talking about. Marcus is nowhere around. He should be the one sitting here dealing with this. I told Marcus that it didn't make any sense for him to buy Markie those one hundred and fifty dollar sneakers at his age anyway. The way these kids fight and kill each other over sneakers, it just wasn't worth it.

"Why didn't you just ignore him?" I ask knowing Jesus would want me to ask that. However, I knew Markie would look at me like I was crazy.

"*Ignore him?* I'm not ignoring him Ma. He's just a little punk anyway." Markie says looking like his father whenever he gets mad. Maybe it was better that his father wasn't around to hear this. I start to call Marcus, but all he would have done was ask Markie to show him what boxing combination he used. Besides, Marcus was the last person I felt like talking to right now anyway.

"That's not the point Markie," I say as I sit at the bottom of the stairs kicking off my favorite closed toe Via Spiga heels that hurt my feet. I can almost hear my toes screaming 'we're free!' just as soon as my shoes are off. "Maybe ignoring him would have saved you from getting suspended. You were just suspended last month for getting into it with some other little boy and now you're missing another three days of school."

"He came at me first, Ma. I'm not gonna let nobody treat me like no chump and take nothing from me. I don't care who it is. All he was doing was showing off in front of his friend."

"So then you showed off in front of yours and look where it got you. Boy, go on upstairs to your room."

"Why do I have to go to my room?"

"Because I said so, that's why!"

"But he started it. I was acting in my own self defense, Ma!"

"Marcus, Jr., get your butt upstairs, *now*!"

He picks up his book bag and stomps up the stairs mumbling something I can't make out.

"What did you say?"

"What? I didn't say anything." He says innocently.

Now I have to go up to the school and deal with this mess. I'm so tired of going up to the school for Lil'Markie that I can scream. If it wasn't his grades, it was his behavior.

After making Jordan a sandwich, I ask Summer to keep an eye on him and I go to my bedroom to grab a few deep breaths. I listen to the telephone messages. There's the usual call from Patrice, a call from Aunt Ruby, and a call from

Tiffany's math teacher. I knew that call would be coming. Tiffany is struggling in geometry so this is probably the "get her a tutor before she fails" call. Another thing on my to-do list I keep forgetting.

I take two Tylenol to ward off my headache and I lay down in the bed for what I believe will only be a few minutes. I hadn't planned to fall asleep, but when I start to play back the day's events in my head, I just doze off into dreamland.

I dreamt of what looked like hundreds of little fish swimming around in this big aquarium. As I press my face against the glass, I see that one of the fish looked familiar, but my vision starts to get fuzzy.

"Mommy! Mommy! Look!" I hear Jordan's voice as he shakes me out of my sleep with his oatmeal cookie breath.

"Oh, ok. What you got there?" I say as I blink my eyes into focus and prop my head up on one elbow to look at a big sheet of construction paper with scribbles on it.

"It's a picture. Guess what it is?" He says as he smacks the piece of construction paper in my face.

"Ooooh, that's nice. I like this. Is this the sky?" I ask trying to look as interested as I can despite the fact that my contact lenses are dry and it's hard for me to make out Jordan's art masterpiece.

"No, it's a car Mommy."

"Oh, yep, now I see. It sure is a car. Can I keep it?"

Jordan shakes his head yes and runs off, crayon in hand. "I'm going to make another one for Daddy!" I hear him say happily as he hops down the steps.

"Hey, Mommy," Summer says as she kisses me on my cheek and sits next to me on the bed. "Are you sick?" Summer is the little nurse of the family. Always concerned when someone isn't feeling well.

"Naw, baby. Mommy was just getting a little rest." I say as I lift up out of bed. Rest and relaxation time are over. It's time to start dinner. Before long, it will be time to leave for rehearsal. I am truly looking forward to singing and getting my mind off of today's craziness. "How was school?" I yawn as I brush my half permed-half nappy roots back into a ponytail. I laugh to myself as I think of Patrice making fun of my hair always being in a ponytail.

"It was good. Guess what? Ms. Fitzpatrick is having a baby." She says with a big smile. Ms. Fitzpatrick is Summer's art teacher. She had been trying to have a baby for a while now. Seems God has finally blessed her womb. That must have been what the fish dream was all about. I got the dream gift from my grandmother. Whenever someone in the family dreams of fish it means somebody in the family or close to the family is pregnant. So it was Ms. Fitzpatrick. "That's nice sweetie." I say, "Go on downstairs and make sure Jordan is alright. I'll be down in a minute."

"Ok, and don't forget I need you to help me practice my spelling words."

"Ok, let Mommy change first. I'll meet you downstairs, okay?"

I change into a pair of jeans and a sweatshirt and return phone calls as I work up some fried chicken, broccoli, sweet potatoes and macaroni and cheese in the kitchen. I save the call to Tiffany's math teacher for last.

"Hello?"

"Hello, Mrs. Thornton?"

"Yes?"

"This is Tyanne Miller. Tiffany's mom. You called?"

"Well, yes. How are you?"

"I'm good. Yourself?"

"I'm good. Has Tiffany talked to you?"

"About math, yes, she has. I know she's struggling. I do intend to get a tutor."

"No not about math, about a note that she had written?"

"No. What note?"

"Well, let me begin by saying, aside from being a teacher, I am also a parent and I felt that I needed to share this with you. During lunch today in the cafeteria there was this note being passed around. Tiffany intended for her friend Danita to get it. Instead, one of our male students snatched it and started running around the cafeteria. Well,

Tiffany chased him and started yelling for him to give her back the note. She was pulling on him and yelling and screaming as he attempted to read the note. That's when I saw them and I took the note from him. Well, that is when Tiffany became irate with me and asked could she have her note back. I told her no she could not have the note since they had been so disruptive. She demanded that I give her the note back saying that it belonged to her and I had no right to take her note. That is when I told her that I would not be returning it and that I would be contacting her parents to let you know of the situation."

"Uh-huh. So what does this note say?" I ask.

"In the note Tiffany explains how she has been throwing up in the mornings. How she would soon be making an appointment for an abortion and that you still had no idea that she was pregnant."

"Oh, no, God no…" I can barely stand. I notice Summer look at me, so I walk upstairs to the bedroom and close the door.

"I'm sorry. I wanted to call you in and talk to you personally, but I felt that you should know as soon as possible. I just feel that this is so serious. I… "

"Yes, it is and I appreciate you calling me when you did." I say as I try hard to maintain my composure, not knowing what else to say. I'm beyond stunned.

"I'm a parent myself and I know how devastated I would be receiving this kind of news." Says Mrs. Thornton, "It seems no matter how much talking and teaching we do they are still going to find a way to do what they want."

"Mrs. Thornton, I really appreciate your call."

"Have a blessed evening Mrs. Miller,"

"Thank you. You too. "

I hang up the phone and cover my mouth. I feel sick.

Tiffany is pregnant. I feel myself taking short, choppy breaths. I go into the bathroom, cut on the fan to cut down on some of the noise, and bawl like a baby.

How can Tiffany be pregnant?

Why, Lord? No, not why, how? When? How did I miss

this one? Jesus, please help me. Tell me where I went wrong with Tiffany? I raised her in the Word. I drilled Your Word into her. I told her about the consequences of sex. She knows all about pregnancy, AIDS, Your covenant. God, I was her Sunday school teacher! Was I just talking for my health? Not, my baby. Please, not my baby. Help me understand, Lord. What are You trying to teach me in all of this? I know with everything comes a lesson. I can't even begin to comprehend this one.

When I hear the front door open and close downstairs, I wipe my eyes and try to pull myself together just in case it's Tiffany. From the sound of the footsteps climbing the stairs, I realize that it's Marcus. I sit up in bed and look at him as if we have just had a death in the family.

"What's wrong with you?" Marcus asks. "Look, if it's about that situation with Mocha… "

"Marcus, I could care less about Mocha. Tiffany is pregnant." I say as I walk into the bathroom and throw water on my face trying to rinse away all the hurt, pain and confusion. The tears won't stop.

"What? How do you know she's pregnant?"

"Her teacher called. There was this note that Tiffany wrote to Danita but the teacher got it and read it. Supposedly she's going to be scheduling an abortion soon."

"Where is she?" Marcus asks looking like he's ready to hurt up something or somebody.

"She hasn't gotten home yet." I say as I sit on the bed with my arms folded. There's so much for Marcus and I to talk about and the list just seems to be getting longer and longer. *Lord, if a house be divided against itself how can it stand?*

"Did you call Danita's house? Call some of her friend's houses and tell her to get her butt home!"

"Marcus, I will, but you and I need to talk about it first."

"Talk about what? This sure ain't gonna work." Marcus says as he paces the floor. "She's too young to have a baby. She hasn't even finished high school yet."

I knew instantly where the conversation was headed. This is where my spiritual beliefs kick in and I have to fight the enemy for all I'm worth. Lord knows I never thought I would have to even think about what we would do if Tiffany got pregnant. But ready or not, this is the real deal.

"Marcus, she's not having an abortion." I say as I close the bedroom door and turn on the television to try and muffle out our voices. I knew nosey rosy Summer was trying to listen.

"Oh, you're really tripping now. You know Tiffany is too young to raise a child. I want my daughter to finish school and have a chance to have a good life. I'm not letting her ruin her life with no baby!"

"Marcus, I hear what you're saying and I agree with you. She is too young. But she's not alone in this" I say calmly, surprising even myself. "And it's deeper than that. This is a human life we're talking about. Having an abortion is nothing short of murder. And aside from that, an abortion is not just some simple procedure Marcus. Do you know how many young girls die from abortions? She could even destroy her chances of getting pregnant whenever she does get married."

"You had an abortion. You turned out alright. Why does she have to be any different? Huh?"

I can't believe he said that. He went right to the jugular.

"Look, Marcus, Tiffany doesn't have to go through what I went through. And whether or not you realize it, I still have emotional scars from those abortions. But you wouldn't understand, so we'll leave that alone. But what I do want you to understand is that it's about more than her health, it's also about her soul. We can't allow her to commit murder and kill this baby. This is a human life we're talking about."

"Here you go with that religious stuff. Don't nobody wanna hear that right now Tyanne. My children are going to be successful in life and I'm not going to let one mistake set Tiffany back and her life be messed up forever because you believe that some book you read says she's going to go to hell if she has an abortion. Whatever. This is real life, not some fairy tale. I'm her father and I say she's too young to have a baby and she's not having a baby right now."

That's when I shut down and walk out of the bedroom. I can't take anymore. It's like arguing with satan himself. I walk to the kitchen and check on the food. I know the kids heard everything, but it really doesn't matter. It's happening and it isn't going away.

Then I hear the front door open.

At first I figure it's Marcus leaving until I hear the rubber bottom of sneakers. It's Tiffany.

I ask the Holy Spirit to give me the words as Marcus and I meet her in the front room. As she takes off her puffy ski coat, the first thing I do is glance at her stomach but she's dressed in a jersey, so I can't see anything. Come to think of it, all she's been wearing lately are jerseys and sweatshirts.

She searches our faces and sits on the couch. She knows we know. She sits on the couch and puts her face in her hands.

Marcus sits on one side of her and I sit on the other. He nods at me to begin talking.

"Why Tiffany?" I ask. I already know that she doesn't have the answer to that question.

The room is silent with the exception of Tiffany's sniffles. Until finally she says, with what I detect as a little sarcasm in her voice, "Ma, I didn't plan on getting pregnant. It just happened."

"It just happened? It doesn't just happen. It happened because you let some trifling little boy tell you anything to get into your little panties. So had you even considered what you were going to do if you were to end up pregnant? You did realize that getting pregnant was a possibility, didn't you?"

She doesn't answer. She just hunches her shoulders. Now, that makes me angry. Hunching shoulders means you could care less. You can say whatever comes to your mind, but don't hunch your shoulders at me. I can't stand that.

"Man, forget all this," Marcus butts in. "We're going to call the doctor so she can get rid of it, that's what we're going to do first thing in the morning. Ain't no way she's having a baby at sixteen. No way."

I hate the fact that Marcus and I have totally different views as parents. It frustrates me even more that our differences are playing out in front of Tiffany. We haven't even had a chance to discuss it fully.

"Tiffany, what are you going to do?" I ask. She hunches her shoulders again. She has one more time to hunch her shoulders.

I walk over to Tiffany and grab her chin between my thumb and fingers, "Look, you're not stupid. You had all the answers when you lay down with whoever you laid down with. Tiffany, you're not going to sit in my face and play dumb. I asked you what you were going to do?"

She looks at her father and then drops her eyes and says, "I want to have an abortion."

From the corner of my eye, I see Marcus fold his arms in a spirit of ill victory. He doesn't smile, but I know my husband. He's relieved.

"Ma, I know how you feel about abortions." Tiffany says. "But this is my life and I'm not ready to have a child."

I shake my head as my eyes fill with tears. "But you're ready to have sex, get pregnant and kill one though."

This whole day has had my head spinning. It's already six o'clock. I had to be at rehearsal in an hour. I get up from the couch, slip on my sneakers, coat and grab my purse and keys.

"Where are you going?" Marcus asks which makes me even angrier that he even has to ask. "Rehearsal Marcus. I told you that already."

I get in the car and pull off leaving a loud screech. I hadn't planned on the screech, but in all honesty I'm feeling real Thelma and Louise-ish.

CHAPTER EIGHT
Marcus

"Daddy, is Mommy coming back?" Jordan asks me as he stands in the window and watches his crazy mother screech from the driveway.

"Yea, Lil' man, your mommy will be back. She's just going to choir rehearsal. Come on and finish eating your dinner."

I call Tiffany to come downstairs and join us. Just because she was going through her situation didn't mean she couldn't sit down and have dinner with the family. She said she wasn't hungry; I make her a plate and tell her to come and sit down at the table anyway.

I can't remember the last time we all sat down at the table to eat dinner together. I mean there have been the pizza dinners after Lil' Markie's games, but I'm usually out at the club around this time. Although I would have to go back and check on the club later, I couldn't leave before first getting the kids situated with dinner and baths before bed.

As we eat in silence, I sneak a peak around the table and look at my children - my beautiful, healthy children, who I love with all of my heart. I think about how my own father must be sorry he missed out on moments like this.

"Marcus, did you tell Dad that you were suspended for fighting today?" Summer says, breaking the silence and spoiling the moment.

"Shut up! Why are you always running your mouth?" Lil Markie gets up and almost pushes Summer out of her chair.

"Hey! Don't push your sister like that boy! Sit your tail down and finish eating your dinner before I get my belt. What were you fighting for anyway?"

"This bamma tried to take my sneakers." Markie said with his forehead all crunched up. "I ain't having it Dad."

I had to pause a moment. One, because Lil' Markie don't weigh nothing but a few pounds and always trying to be hard. That's funny to me. Secondly, I had to put myself in his shoes. If somebody tried to take my sneakers I would defend myself, too. The boy can't help it. He's a Miller from the blood.

"Did the other boy get suspended?" I ask.

"Yea, he got suspended."

I nod slightly and continue to eat. I catch the look on Summer's face. The same look Tyanne gives me when she doesn't approve. My baby girl would understand one day that boys have it different from girls. For some reason, dudes love to try other dudes to see who is the toughest and the roughest. I'll raise my boys to stand up for themselves and never fear anyone.

"Tiffany, are you having a baby?" Summer breaks the silence again. Tiffany doesn't answer. She just looks at Summer as if she wants to beat her butt.

"Summer, won't you shut up and mind your business," Lil' Markie says. "Dad, can you tell Summer to stop getting in everybody's business? We're trying to eat. Dag."

"Well, this is what people do at dinner time." Summer says with her grown up attitude. "They make conversation, so I'm making conversation. So are you Tiffany?"

"No, Tiffany is not having a baby." I butt in. "And we can find other things to talk about."

"Like what?" Summer asks.

"Like, are you ready for your spelling bee?" I ask.

"Yes, and I'm going to win, too." Summer says as she takes a napkin and wipes Jordan's face. A Tyanne move if I ever saw one.

"Now, that's what I like to hear." I say.

"Are you going to win money for this spelling bee or something? It's all you talk about." Lil' Markie asks with his forehead crunched up.

"No, you don't win money, but you win a scholarship for college. That's more valuable than a little bit of money." Summer says with her head cocked to the side trying to irritate Markie.

"Nothing is more valuable than money, right Dad?" Lil' Markie asks.

My heart drops.

"Right dad?" Lil' Markie asks again.

"No, Markie," I say. "That's not right. Your life is way more important than money. Your family is more important than money. You remember that, alright?" I grab his chin and look into his eyes. "Know that life is more important than any amount of money, alright?"

He shakes his head yes. I can tell he is a little uncomfortable with my mood change, but I realize at that moment, that Marcus Jr. understands clearly what he sees and not what I want him to believe. That comment made me break out in a cold sweat.

The table falls silent again. That is until my pager goes off. The kids take it as their opportunity to exit the table. Tiffany is the first to leave the table, and then Markie Jr. and Summer follow.

"Make sure ya'll take your showers." I yell behind them as they run upstairs.

I pull Jordan from the booster seat and grab my pager. I don't recognize the number.

I take Jordan upstairs to my bedroom, run his bath water and put a Sponge Bob Square Pants tape into the VCR to keep him company as I call the number back.

"Yeah? You page somebody?" I ask after hearing a female's voice say hello.

"Hey, Marcus. It's Mocha."

"Hey. What's up?" As surprised as I am to hear her voice this time of night, I make it my business to sound like I'm not.

"I don't mean to bother you, but are you at the club?"

"Naw, not right now. Why, what's up?"

"I just realized I left my briefcase at Champions. I remember leaving it in the office when your wife got my nerves all jumbled up." Mocha laughs. I was glad she was able to laugh about it. I still hadn't had the chance to talk to Tyanne and let her know how foul she was to treat Mocha the way she did.

"Oh, okay. Well, I'm going back there later to check the club. I'll look for it and hold it for you."

"Actually, I need it tonight. I'm catching a plane in the morning for a day trip to Philly and my tickets are in the briefcase."

"Oh, so you gonna come and pick it up tonight?"

"Marcus, you know my transportation situation. If I could, I would." Mocha says. "I hate to ask, but do you think it all possible you could bring it to me?"

"Tonight?"

"Yes. Or unless you're going to bring it to me before my 5 o'clock flight in the morning?"

"Aw, naw, that's too early. I'll bring it to you tonight." That was the least I could do. I mean she was still going to help out at Champions even after that craziness with Tyanne.

"Oh, and I'm at my girlfriend's house." Mocha said. "She lives a few blocks from Bone on 5th Street. Her house number is 564."

"Alright. I have to give my son a bath and get him to bed. Give me about an hour or so."

"Thanks Marcus. I really appreciate it."

After giving Jordan his bath and putting him in the bed with Tiffany, I take a quick shower and put on some fresh gear.

The whole time I'm thinking about Mocha.

CHAPTER NINE
Tyanne

Neither Fred Hammond's "Inner Court" CD or the jazz radio station are enough to calm my nerves by the time I arrive at the studio. I pull up and I sit in the car a few minutes debating whether or not to go in. I know I look a hot mess. After all, I cried the whole drive.

I cut on the light in the car and check my face in the mirror. My eyes are red and the bags under my eyes are sagging. Nile will probably think I've been in a fight. I pull out my foundation sponge and swipe it across my face a few times in an attempt to liven it up a bit. Come on, Tyanne. God's got it. Stay focused and do what you came to do. The devil is a liar.

The studio is located in a three story building on a side street in Southwest D.C. I personally think the building can use a little Pine Sol, but other than that it's decent. I pass on Nile's instructions to call him before coming up. I'm a homegrown DC girl who is more than use to the junkies and homeless standing in front of entranceways begging.

I take the stairs rather than the loud, clanking claustrophobia-causing box that building management has been passing off as an elevator. I trust God, but I wasn't about to trust the elevator. Soon after I ring the doorbell, I hear footsteps approach the door and it opens to a cheerful Nile Rivers.

"Hey," Nile greets me with the same enthusiasm he always does. Just what I need to get my mind off of the craziness I'd just left.

"Hey Nile. How are you?" I say as I try to force the same enthusiasm and hope he doesn't detect the big hole in my soul.

"Great. Can I get you anything? Water? Tea?" Nile asks as he grabs my coat and hangs it in the closet. Wearing a pair of jeans, a Coogi sweater, his fine brown hair tapered against his caramel latte skin and a whiff of wonderfully pleasant smelling cologne to boot, one can't help but take in the handsomeness of this man.

"No, no I'm fine. Thanks." I say as I follow Nile to the recording area of the studio and quickly bind any thoughts of attraction past, present and future.

I love coming to the studio. The whole vibe always puts me in a place of serenity. Sounds of John Coltrane fill the atmosphere and pictures of jazz greats line the walls. Duke Ellington. Miles Davis. Sarah Vaughn. Nina Simone. Nile and I have talked on many occasions and he has made it clear that his life's crusade is to bring the music of jazz to the church. "They can call it Christian jazz, Gospel jazz, whatever they want to, but jazz is jazz." He had said once, "Singers sing unto the Lord and I play my keyboard and piano unto the Lord. No difference. Jazz music is beautiful in and of itself, but the sound is even more amazing when it's created with God's presence and anointing."

I agree wholeheartedly. I love jazz. Although Nile's taste is more old school jazz, I appreciate the contemporary sounds of Boney James, Alex Bugnon and Kirk Whalum or the solo compositions of Cassandra Wilson, Diane Reeves and Nnena Freelon. Whenever I'm not listening to gospel music, I'm listening to jazz music. There is something about jazz music that can lift me up when I'm down and give me peace when I'm feeling unsettled.

For years, I thought my love for jazz was just an acquired taste that I had happened upon. I would learn from my Aunt Ruby that my great-great-great grandmother was a jazz vocalist in her day. Aunt Ruby told me she took a lot of heat from her parents about her love for jazz. They questioned her spirituality and told her that jazz was the devil's music. Aunt Ruby said my great-great-great grandmother no doubt loved the Lord but she would not give up singing jazz. I was blown away by her story as I considered the church today still hasn't embraced jazz music.

Seeing the instruments and my fellow Windstorm band members, my heart begins to flutter. I am so ready to sing. Though it feels bittersweet that this is our last rehearsal, I have a strong feeling that God is going to do something with this collaboration that is beyond us all. The sadness I felt during the drive is now being replaced with an intense desire to sing and give glory unto God. If only for a moment, I am ready to forget about my troubles and I am ready to sing His praises.

After I hug and greet the band members, we join hands for prayer.

"This is it, guys," Nile says after the prayer, beaming like he has just come off the mountaintop. "Let's do the daggone thing for our glorious King."

Everyone takes their position. I put on the headphones and close my eyes. In spite of the five piece band, I pretend there is nobody in the room but me and Jesus.

I hear the music as I have heard it at previous rehearsals, but this time, the sound is different. This time my heart yearns to yield to His worship. I wait for the place in the song where the saxophone and violin fade and I chime in:

Loving You is all I know to do
Your Spirit holds me
You console me
You let me know that everything will be alright
O Lord, I honor You
I magnify You
For the rest of my days,
I will give Your name the praise

The next sound in the room is the skillful, mesmerizing sound of Nile's piano. The volume heightens and the melody is heavenly. After a few more verses, I continue with the hook as the saxophone plays and matches my every word, "I will give Your name the praise…. I will give Your name the praise… "

Over and over again, I sing these six words. Each instrument finds its place in the groove and our sounds intertwine to bring about a sweet, anointed melody of worship. After a time of raised hands and shouting praises unto the Lord, the musicians can no longer play, I can no longer sing and we all lay prostrate as we are overcome by the powerful presence of the Lord. It's the ultimate worship experience indeed. We wrap up the recording of the final studio songs on the CD and we all agree that we have rendered our most excellent worship and the CD will be a godly masterpiece.

Afterwards, Nile and the violinist Nakeeta arrange a beautiful dinner celebration for the group. There are catered Caribbean dishes, fruit drinks and enough sweets to open a bakery. Nile has our musical masterpiece playing in the background as we delight ourselves in eating and fellowship.

"You were wonderful." Nile says to me as he bites into a jerk chicken wing. You would think he hadn't eaten in weeks. Nile is a Caribbean boy, so half of the dishes on the table are super spicy.

"Thanks to you," I say as I enjoy my delicious rice peas and banana coconut bread.

"Me? I don't think so my sister," Nile says. "Your voice is a gift from God Almighty. Truly."

"Yes, but you gave me an opportunity to take it to another level. And for that, I am grateful."

"And I am grateful that you said yes. It would not have been the same without you."

Nile is my definition of a mighty man of valor. I remember when we first started recording, I had to fast and pray from the strong attraction I had for him. There's nothing more attractive than a handsome, God-fearing, worshipping man of God. If Nile was attracted to me, he never let on. He has always treated me with the respect a brother would a sister. I thank God for that. For there were many times when I was so weak in the flesh, all he had to do was blow on me and I would have said, 'yes, take me!' The truth is the truth. But I thank God for deliverance. I thank God for His word and serious prayer warriors like Patrice who not only prayed for me but told me she would kick my butt if I didn't get over myself.

The evening rounds out with eating, laughing and story telling. Russ, the bass guitarist must have been a comedian in another life. He has us laughing until we are bent over crying from his funny church tale experiences. He tells a story about how he somehow slipped and fell while playing his bass guitar during a funeral service and some of the family members of the deceased started laughing at him. He says he didn't know whether to laugh with them or just keep a straight face. He says he gave a face that was a combination of a smile and a serious expression. He keeps describing the face over and over which has us bent over in laughter. Russ has eyes that poke out like Chris Tucker. I laugh until I'm dizzy.

"Hear ye, hear ye. Can I have your attention please?" Nile stands in the middle of the floor hitting his coconut smoothie filled glass. "Before you hear it through the grapevine, we wanted you all to be the first to know." Nakeeta moves in closer and Nile grabs her hand. "I have asked this beautiful woman to marry me and she said yes."

Everyone claps and whistles with excitement as Nile seals it with a kiss on Nakeeta's cheek. "We just finished our counseling classes with Pastor and she has decided she still wants me. And so that she doesn't get away, we're getting married tonight."

We all look at each other and hope Nile is just kidding. He busts out laughing, "I'm just kidding. We've planned a June wedding."

We all clap and whistle some more.

"Now, tell us how you were able to keep that secret from getting out in church." Boyd, the drummer asks. Everyone laughs.

"Now ain't that the truth." Nile says. "Well, I can only say we have a Pastor who is a man of integrity and we asked that he not share it with anyone. Seems he kept his word."

Everyone nods and says amen in agreement. Pastor is a man I too regard as honest and trustworthy. Since the time I shared with him about the marital problems between Marcus and I, he has only encouraged me and I've never heard anything I've shared with him over the pulpit or spoken through the congregation.

"I'm not only sharing this with you all because I want you all to play and sing at my wedding, hint hint," Nile says smiling and looks at me when he says the word sing, "but everyone standing here is married. Some of you are newly married; some of you have been married since the Rock Ages. I want you to take a moment to pour into our lives right now with words of wisdom on the secret to long lasting love. We want the good, the bad and the ugly, don't we baby?"

Nakeeta smiles, "Yes, we do."

I like Nakeeta. From the first time I met her, I noticed the quiet, confident spirit about her. She and Nile will make a wonderful couple.

"Come on. Each person, please stand and share with us what it takes to keep it together."

My heart sinks.

Keep it together? I didn't have the secret, the recipe or any words of wisdom in my heart about keeping a marriage together. All I was feeling concerning marriage was frustration, confusion and a strong desire to end it all. For so long, I kept up a good front in church that all was fine at home and I wanted to keep it that way. Especially since this was such a special time for Nile and Nakeeta. The last thing I want to do is spoil it with my marital mess.

One by one, each musician stands and begins sharing. Boyd, the drummer says that unconditional love, prayer, and forgiveness are the key to everlasting love. He also shares that he and his wife had a rough spot in their marriage last year and decided that their love was stronger 'than he that was in the world' and they chose to hang in there.

Everyone shouts hallelujah and amen. Russ grabs Boyd's drumsticks to do a drum roll knowing he has not a clue as to how to play the drums. Russ then shares that although he has only been married for two years that he has learned the key to everlasting love is lots of laughter, lots of sex and having a bass guitar around. This sends everyone into a laughing frenzy, except for me. I am nervous and at a loss for words.

"I impart to you both to be humble," Rick, the saxophonist says, "Humble yourselves even when you know you haven't done anything. Your humility will save your marriage and will in turn humble your partner as your partner witnesses your quiet strength in times of conflict. I got eighteen years of marriage to back me up. All that going back and forth trying to prove whose right ain't worth it. Humility will win every time and put the devil to shame. Mark my words."

"I know that's right." Russ says.

The room falls silent after all of the whispers of amen and hallelujahs are done. It's my turn and all eyes are on me. My eyes begin to water as I think about what my flesh wants to share as opposed to what the Holy Spirit is encouraging me to say. I can be disobedient and give a polished fake bit or I can allow the Holy Spirit to expose me and use me the way the Holy Spirit wants.

"It's alright. Take your time." Boyd says.

"That's right." Nakeeta adds.

When I hear these comforting voices, my emotions grow stronger, my chin quivers and the tears roll even faster down my cheeks. I find it difficult to speak, but eventually the words come.

"Nile and Nakeeta, I am so happy for you. The love I see on you is beautiful and oh how I pray you many, many years of holy matrimony. Yet as I stand here listening and thinking about what I want to say, I stand with a broken heart tonight. I'm really going through. I wasn't going to share because I didn't want to spoil this moment for you… "

"You're among family that loves you," Nakeeta says as she moves to me and grabs my hand in hers, "Speak your heart sister."

"And Nile did say he wanted the good, bad and the ugly." Russ says.

Nobody laughs outwardly, but I'm sure they are laughing inside at Russ who always looks for the humor in everything. I smile at Russ to let him know that I appreciate his gift of humor even at such an awkward and emotional moment.

"You all know I am married to a man who doesn't have a relationship with the Lord. It's been hard ya'll, I won't lie. There is so much going on... for so long I have prayed and prayed... and just the other day, I decided I was going to leave him. Yet as I stand in this anointed room filled with Holy Spirit filled friends who believe in the miraculous power of God, I'm humbled... I'm convicted... and I want to ask that you pray much for me, my marriage and my family. I do want my marriage... I really do..." And with that, I can't speak another word. I begin to cry like a baby. Nakeeta embraces me and whispers over and over in my ear, "God is able. God is able... "

"Come on family. Let us pray for our sister and her family." Nile says.

Everyone places their hands on my back and my head and the prayer begins. It is a powerful prayer of reconciliation, restoration, forgiveness and God's mercy. Those who know the prayer language of tongues began to speak as the Holy Spirit gives them utterance, including myself. We pray aloud until a sweet, unified hush falls upon the room. It's such an amazing experience. It brings an unexplainable joy in my heart and a huge smile on my face. I know at this moment that the Spirit of the Lord is in this place.

As we all go around the room and give each other holy hugs, Nile stands before me with his hands on my shoulders and says to me, "Promise me no matter what, you'll trust God and let Him work it out?"

"I promise." And I mean it. It's a heart commitment that I'm making not only to Nile, but to myself and to God.

* * *

Riding home, I can't stop smiling. The joy I have on the inside, I never want it to go away. I truly believe I received my breakthrough and that everything is going to be alright. All of the anger, resentment and doubt I felt earlier has now been replaced with an overwhelming and unexplainable hope. I can't wait to get home to Marcus. I need to let him know that I love him and that no matter what; I am willing to work it out. I've decided I will no longer worry. I will refocus my attention on the Lord and allow Him to deal with Marcus, Tiffany – everything. I need to get back to my first love - total worship unto God. I need to get back to loving and trusting God with my whole, heart, mind and soul and believe that He really can work it out.

Lord, forgive me for being double minded and for doubting. Right now, I put all trust and faith in You, I believe that You are able to do exceeding and abundantly above all I could ever ask or think according to the power that works within me. Have Your way in our lives O Lord. In Jesus' precious name I pray, Amen.

CHAPTER TEN
Marcus

When I arrive at Mocha's to drop off her briefcase, it's a little on the late side, but when I pull up to the house I can see the lights on through the window. I pull the door knocker a few times. A short, big boned girl, holding a glass of wine answers the door. She looks like she painted all her clothes on. I'll never understand why chunky girls wear everything so tight. Shortie was packing though.
"Hey, is Mocha in?" I ask.
"Hello, Marcus. I'm Candace. Come on in."
From my view, I can see a small party going on in the living room. Lots of giggling and Mary J. Blige's, "I'm Going Down" catches my attention as shortie with the glass of wine leads me instead into a small room off the foyer. As soon as I sit on the couch, Mocha sways into the room. Baby looks like a supermodel coming around the corner with her midriff tee-shirt, no bra, tight jeans and a wine cooler. Just as I start to get up from the couch, she sits down beside me.
"Thanks for coming," Mocha smiles. "I couldn't get very far without the plane tickets."
"Right, right," I say as I hand her the briefcase. "So, what are you having a little party tonight?" I nod in the direction of Mary J. Blige's voice and the giggling girls.
"No, just a little get together with some friends. Would you like a beer or a glass of wine?"
"Naw, I don't drink."
"Neither do I. Candace just broke up with her boyfriend and she wants all of us to get drunk with her." Mocha says giggling.
From the way her eyes are slanting and all the giggling she's doing, it seems she was already a little on the tipsy side.

"I really appreciate you taking the time to bring my briefcase." Mocha says, "No matter what they say about you, you're alright." Mocha says as she smiles and takes a swig from her cooler.

"Is that right?"

"Yes, it is." Mocha says and keeps putting that sexy smile on me. "Tyanne is really lucky to have a brother like you. You're handsome. You're a smart, businessman and a great father. And you're sexy to top it off."

I laugh. She sure knows what to say to make a brother poke his chest out.

"And whoever dude is he's lucky to have a girl like you."

"There you go thinking you know about me. There is no dude."

"What? No dude? So is there another girl?"

Mocha laughs out. I'm glad she does. I never could understand that lesbian stuff. Not for the sisters anyway. What for? When you got brothers walking around looking as good as me?

"No. I'm not a lesbian." Mocha says, "I'm just not seeing anyone right now. And unless I can find somebody like you, I'll just wait it out."

Now baby knew good and well she was coming on to me. And to be honest, the way she was looking at me, I was getting kind of stirred up.

"So what's taking you to Philly tomorrow?"

She looks at me like she forgot she had told me about the plane tickets. It must be the cooler. "Oh, I'm riding up for my little brother's high school graduation."

"Oh, I see."

"Don't worry," Mocha says, "I see that look on your face. It's only for the day. Actually, I'll be back in town tomorrow evening. I'll be ready bright and early Thursday to take care of the paperwork you wanted me to take care of for you."

"What? You know how to read minds now?"

"No. You just have one of those honest faces." Mocha

says, "You can't hide what you're thinking."
"Is that right?"
"Yep."
"So what I'm thinking now?"
"That you want to kiss me."
"What?" I give her my smooth laugh and lick my lips sexier than LL Cool J ever could.
"Stop pretending. I know you're attracted to me Marcus. And I'm definitely attracted to you."

Before I can even think of what to say or how to react, Mocha slides closer to me and starts kissing me all across my face and then her lips touch mine. Part of me wants her to stop, but most of me just wants her to keep on going. I feel my body moving forward, like I'm suspended in air or something. I give in a little, but not too much. It's taking all I have to keep my hands off of her.

"I want you, Marcus." She says as she stands, closes the door and pulls her shirt over her head, confirming my suspicion that she isn't wearing a bra. From there, she steps out of her jeans and walks up to me with nothing on but a thong. Baby is sexy. No diggity. No doubt.

"You want me, too. Don't you?" She says as she sways her hips to the music, grabs both my hands and pulls me up to her.

I'm a can of slime. I can't move or speak. Mocha has me under her control. Control I can't remember losing like this in a long, long time. After removing my shirt, she slowly unzips my jeans and the secret is out that I want her, too. Soon my pants make their way to my ankles and my mind starts to race. I'm thinking that if I don't move or participate that I really have nothing to do with what's going on. In actuality, she's taking advantage of me.

Just as Mocha starts to kiss me again, I hear a sound that shakes me back to reality - a sound that drowns out Mary J singing "I'm Going Down" - a sound that reminds me of who I am and where I am - the one sound I don't want to hear at this moment.

It's my pager ringing at my ankles.

The pager I now wish I had turned off but didn't. I knew I needed to keep it on just in case the kids needed to reach me. As Mocha continues to kiss me all over my body, my mind starts a fight with my body and then from out of nowhere my heart gets in on the fight. And for a moment when I look down at Mocha, I think I see Tyanne. I'm tripping and I know I haven't had anything to drink. I step back from Mocha, pull up my pants and reach for my pager.

It's my home telephone number. Something is wrong.

When I left home, Tyanne was at rehearsal and the kids were asleep. Something has to be wrong.

"Can I use your phone?" I ask already dialing before Mocha can answer.

"Sure. Go ahead," Mocha says sarcastically as she stands in the middle of the floor and puts her clothes back on.

"Hello?" It's Tyanne's voice.

"Hey, what's up?" I ask nervously, hoping I sound relaxed.

"What's up with you?" Not only is it Tyanne, she has a voice that I haven't heard in a long time. It's actually her sexy, sweet I-want-to-make-up voice. Man, oh man.

"I'm over Bone's cousin house watching the game. Everything alright?"

Now that isn't a lie. After all, Mocha is Bone's cousin.

"Yes, everything is fine. The kids are asleep. I was hoping you would be here when I got home."

"Yeah, after I went by to check on the club I stopped over here to watch the game. Everything alright? How did rehearsal go?"

"It was beautiful, Marcus. It was life changing actually."

"So ya'll ready for tomorrow night then, huh?" Mocha rolls her eyes as she leaves the room and slams the door.

"Yep, we're good and ready." Tyanne says, "So what time will you be home? I want to talk to you."

"About what?"

"About us. About what's on my heart. Things."

"Okay. I'll be home after I finish chillin' here."

"Alright, I'll see you when you get here. Don't be too late Marcus."

"Alright. I won't."

"I love you."

"I love you, too."

This is one of those times that I want to call on Gazoo from The Flintstones so he can work his magic and blink me out of the house. I also want Gazoo to blink away what almost happened between me and Mocha. But I know that's not going to happen.

After I fix my clothes, I walk out to the foyer and peep around to the living room for Mocha. She's sitting at the table with her friends laughing, talking and sipping wine, obviously trying hard to ignore me. Eventually she gives me a look that tells me to get out of her face, get out of the house and that she isn't about to walk me to the door.

I show myself out the door, get in my Porsche and screech off. Yeah, screeching was a little on the bamma side, but it was my way of telling Mocha that getting out of her face and even her life was the best thing that could happen to me right about now.

* * *

There was no way I was going straight home after having some naked chick all over me. I drop by Champions, slide through the back entrance and take a shower. I always keep extra clothes; you never know when you're going to need them. Smelling fresh and looking like a million bucks in a loose silk shirt and a pair of baggy slacks, I make my entrance into the club area. It's live and popping just as I expect. Dancing, drinking, loud talking and laughter – everybody is having a good time. Chuck Brown and the Soul Searchers are playing tonight. Chuck is tearing it up with his horn. The crowd is feeling it:

"Chuck Baby don't give uh!"

"Say what?"

"Chuck Baby don't give uh!"

I walk through and give dap to the brothers, hugs to the sisters and make my way to the bar where Bone and Phil Perry are sitting.

"What's up, player?" Bone pulls me into his chest, about to smother me with his brotherly love. "Ain't nothing." I say and then reach over and give Phil some dap. Soon after, Phil whispers something in Bone's ear, waves goodbye and walks off. "Alright now" Bone says to Phil.

I give a little nod to Phil as he leaves. "Why he leave when I get here?" I ask Bone.

"Man, what you paranoid? Stop tripping. The brother been here for a while hanging with me. He's on a mission anyway. He told me he's going to have the joint tomorrow, so I'm going to need you to get my money to me."

"That's cool. When you wanna come get it?"

"We can hook up tomorrow. I'll call you."

"Alright. And make it early. You know Tyanne's concert is tomorrow night. You going?"

"All the sexy church ladies gonna be there, you think I ain't?" Bone says, "You never know, I might just mess around and get saved up in that piece player." Bone looks at me and gives his Mack daddy grit as he nods his head to the music.

"Not only that," I say, "Maybe somebody can lay hands on you and you can lose about two hundred pounds miraculously." I fall out laughing.

"Forget you man" Bone says, takes a sip from his glass and keeps nodding to the music.

I nod along, too. I'm not ready to go home just yet. I need time to get this guilty feeling out my system and any traces of it off my face. I would stay at Champions until I was sure Tyanne was sound asleep.

CHAPTER ELEVEN
Tyanne

Wednesday, February 17

My alarm sounds off at six; I smile as I open my eyes and look to the heavens. This is the day the Lord has made and I am glad to be in it. I have a wonderful feeling that today is going to change the rest of my life forever.

I heard Marcus crawl in the bed at about three in the morning, but I was too tired to roll over and talk about life at that time of morning. I decide I won't be upset that he came home late. Instead I choose to embrace the revelation I received about our marriage at rehearsal. Whenever we do talk, I will let Marcus know that I love him and I want us to work it out. I have reached the conclusion that Marcus' sins are his sins, but he's still my husband and I love him. My heart is willing to love him unconditionally and I will trust God to save Marcus and heal our marriage.

I look over at Marcus who is asleep and snoring and I know talking is the last thing on his mind. The more I look at his smooth, brown body; talking isn't on my mind either. I'm thinking about what this sister taught at a women's conference I attended some time ago. She said having sex with our husbands brings us closer together both physically and spiritually. Not having sex causes an emotional and spiritual separation. She said sometimes during the most stressful and tense moments in a relationship, words have no place and all that is needed is some real, good lovemaking.

It has been quite some time since I've given Marcus some goodies. If the truth be told, just looking at his naturally toned body is turning me on. I pull closer to Marcus and began to run my hands over every inch of his body. And I mean every inch. His body begins to stir and his eyes flicker open. He looks at me and says nothing. I don't say anything either. We just grab one another and allow ourselves to love on each other, nice and slowly. Soon nice and slow becomes Marcus and Tyanne gone wild. We can talk later. Right now, our warm brown bodies clinging together say more than words ever could.

As much as I want to spend the whole day with Marcus, somebody has to get the kids up and off to school. Besides, I have a big night to prepare for. As Marcus dozes off again, I pray, shower, and throw on my fuchsia terry cloth sweat suit and white Adidas. A pony tail will have to do for now. Actually, a pony tail has been doing it for a while now. I am so glad to be going to Patrice's shop to get my hair done later.

I call my ob-gyn and I am able to get Tiffany an early morning appointment. As much as I want this whole matter with Tiffany to disappear, it is still very real. And we will see how real it is when we see the doctor this morning.

I get the kids up, fed and dressed and leave a note for Marcus that I'll see him later.

I can't find any words for Tiffany during the ride to the doctor's office. I am still dealing with my own feelings about everything. Still not wanting to believe this is actually happening, ready or not, Tiffany is pregnant. The plan this morning is to have Tiffany examined to find out how far along she is. From there, I can only hope the reality of how much the baby has grown might cause both Marcus and Tiffany to see things differently, to see this as a real baby and not some "thing" we can just throw out with the garbage because the timing is off.

I quickly turn the radio from the station playing Marvin Gaye's "Sexual Healing" to a Christian radio station where they just happen to be talking about the reasons for infertility. I glance at Tiffany every now and then from the corner of my eye to see if she is listening. Her face is the same balled up way it was when she first got in the car.

The doctor's office is only about a half hour away.

When we arrive and sign in, Jill the front desk receptionist greets us with a warm, quiet hello. Jill, along with Dr. Freedman, has seen all of my children from their first hours of life, for their shots, colds, earaches and now – this. Jill understands completely why I am not my cheerful self and keeps small talk to a minimum.

The physician assistant takes Tiffany to the back. She informs me that she will collect urine and blood samples from Tiffany and Dr. Freedman will examine her shortly thereafter. I choose to stay in the waiting room. My days for sitting in the exam room with my Lil' Tiff are apparently over. Lil' Tiff has now graduated to Ms. Grownie status. I grab a magazine and start looking at article headlines and pictures. Even if I want to, my brain can't begin to handle reading an article right now. Though there is an interesting article on "Ten Ways to Drive Him Wild in Bed" that catches my attention.

By the time I read the "Ten Ways" and realize I have only tried maybe three of them at best, the physician assistant leads me back to Dr. Freedman's office. Tiffany is seated in one of the big cherry wood leather chairs with red, puffy eyes. I look at her, wanting desperately to wrap my arms around her, I decide instead to let her deal with her feelings alone.

Dr. Freedman, with his peppered short afro and full beard, swings the door open. Smelling like a big cup of coffee, his burgundy loafers swipe the floor as he sits across from us in the matching cherry wood chair and desk. I feel like I am in the principal's office.

"Tyanne! Long time. How have you been?" Dr. Freeman asks loud and cheerful.

"Hi, Dr. Freedman. I'm good. How are you?" I ask forcing a smile. Dr. Freedman has to know I am not in the mood for all the grinning. He flashes his wide, false front teeth smile at the both of us anyway.

"Oh, I can't complain," He says, "How's the rest of the family?"

"They're good, thanks."

"Well. We've taken all of the tests." He locks his fingers together on his desk and the wide smile caves in. "And based on the results, it looks like we have ourselves a baby here."

The room falls silent as Dr. Freedman looks back and forth from me to Tiffany apparently looking for a response from either of us.

I don't flinch. Tiffany rubs away tears but makes no sound.

Dr. Freedman goes on to explain that Tiffany is about eight weeks into her pregnancy. He gives Tiffany a long schooling about her body, the growth of the baby and tells us to make a follow up appointment on our way out. I am numb and quiet as I walk to the car. Truth has hit me straight in the heart. My baby is having a baby.

When we get in the car, I sit for a moment before I start the ignition. So many thoughts are swirling around in my head. Up until now, I have said as little to Tiffany as possible as my emotions are unstable. I don't want to go off on her, so I just keep quiet and let it pass. Yet I know good and well it's time to move past my selfishness. Questions need answering. There are decisions to be made.

"Ma, I'm going to keep it."

I turn and look at Tiffany. Unable to speak, my eyes beg her to go on.

"I just don't think I can live with the fact that I killed my baby." Tiffany says through sniffles, "A baby that has nothing to do with the choices I made. I don't want to have an abortion. I want to keep my baby."

My God, my dear God. Ok. Praise God for good and moral thinking, but my mind still needed to know why. "Why Tiffany? Why would you have sex knowing all that you know? All that I taught you and you still go out and… "

"Ma, I know I was wrong, okay? I made the wrong choice and I'm going to have to live with this. But I also know that God forgives. I talked to Pastor about it and he told me…"

"Wait a minute. You talked to who? When did you talk to Pastor?"

"I called him last night Ma. I needed somebody to talk to. Somebody to tell me that I wasn't going to hell and that God really does still love me. After I told you, you acted like you hated me." Tiffany says with tears running down her cheeks. I reach in the glove compartment and hand her a few McDonald's napkins to wipe her face.

"Tiffany, I could never hate you. I love you. I just can't understand why. I mean it's just hard for me to accept the fact that you had sex. After the way I raised you. I mean, the least you could have done was use a condom. Ya'll didn't have sense enough to use a condom? You could have caught a disease or anything."

"We did use a condom. It broke." She says and looks out of the window. "Maybe if I had taken birth control pills like the rest of my friends, I wouldn't have got pregnant."

"Tiffany, keeping your legs closed would have stopped you from getting pregnant." I say trying hard not to grow angry again. "And you know what I taught you about birth control pills. The risks far outweigh the advantages."

"Yes, I know. That's why I never took them, but I was really thinking about it."

It's so true. You can talk and teach all you want, but when it's all said and done, we all have free will. Tiffany is a living testament to that truth for sure.

"So who did you have sex with Tiffany?" It could only be Sammy the basketball player or Timothy at church. Those are the only two little boys who call the house. Deep down, I was hoping it was Timothy. He at least knew who God was. Sammy probably hadn't even seen the outside of a church.

"Sammy."

It just keeps getting better. "Has he told his parents?"

"No. He said he wasn't going to tell them until I was sure about what I was going to do."

"Oh, so he's leaving it up to you, huh? Isn't that nice" I say with sarcasm. No matter how hard I try to be sympathetic to this whole thing, the anger just keeps seeping through. "So what are your plans to take care of this baby?"

"Sammy is going to try and get a job where his mother

works. She's been on her job for a long time and Sammy is sure she can get him something. I was going to ask you could you help me get a job where you work. Something I could do after school?" Tiffany looks at me desperately with her beautiful yet sad brown eyes, her face wet with tears.

That's when I break. I reach over, hug her and we both sit in the car and bawl like newborn babies. My baby has made a mistake and now she is trying to survive it and here I am being an angry, unsupportive, stubborn fool. It's not like I haven't been here before myself. The sins of my past are haunting me for sure. I cry for her, I cry for me. I cry for every hurt, heartbreak and disappointment from the past week - actually the past decade.

After pulling myself together, I tell Tiffany that everything is going to work out and we are going to make sure her and the baby are alright. I still can't believe she called Pastor behind my back. Okay, pride shut up. I guess she wouldn't have had to if I would have been there for her when she needed me. Well, I promised her that I would be there for her and that I was taking back everything the devil stole. It certainly isn't going to be easy, but we'll get through it.

"What about Dad?" Tiffany asks as if she's sitting inside my brain. I was thinking the same thing.

"Don't worry about your Dad. God will take care of him."

I have no idea how, but I believe He will.

CHAPTER TWELVE
Marcus

At first, I didn't know if I was dreaming or what. All I knew is if it were a dream, I didn't want to wake up. I remember her sliding her warm, soft body under the covers and her hands were all over me. Rubbing and grabbing everything. I ran my hands across those round curves and big soft bumps that I hadn't touched in what seemed like forever. Man, my wife felt good.

With only having a few hours of sleep, I doze back off. That is until my pager goes off like a smoke alarm. I wake up and Tyanne is gone which makes me wonder real hard as to whether or not our wild thing was a dream. I sit up to go to the bathroom and notice I'm without my underwear. That's proof enough.

Still groggy from her whipping it on me, I stagger to the bathroom and find Tyanne's note and a concert ticket on the toilet:

Hey baby. Gone to get pretty.
Hopefully, I'll see you before tonight.
If not, here's a ticket. Be on time!
You were yummy this morning ☺
Love, Sexy legs.

You was yummy too baby.

My pager goes off again. It's probably Bone's fat butt. I dial the number back.

"Hello?"

"Who 'dis?" I ask.

"It's the girl with the beautiful, sexy body that you were with last night."

It's Mocha. The last person I expect to hear from. She must have a split personality or something. I just knew she was through with me. I need to go ahead and nip this craziness in the bud right now. "Ay, you know what? I gotta apologize about last night… "

"No, need for an apology." She says real sexy like. "I was calling to find out when we could pick back up where we left off?"

"You for real?"

"Yes, I'm for real. I want you Marcus."

"Look, Mocha." I say as I put on my underwear and pace the floor so I can think. "I'm married baby. I'm not trying to… "

"It can be our little secret. If you don't tell, I won't tell."

"Well, put it like this. There won't be anything to tell because me and my wife are working our thing out, alright? So let's just squash whatever that was, alright?"

"No. I don't think so."

"What you mean you don't think so?" I know Mocha isn't trying to go Fatal Attraction on a brother.

"I'm not some freak you can just kick to the curb Marcus."

"I'm not kicking you to the curb." I say trying not to sound too much like a punk. "I'm just not trying to get out on my wife."

"Excuse me, but you already did. I can't wait to see her at the concert tonight and let her know how good you felt the other night. Let her know how I had you out of those Calvin Klein drawers. Mmm good."

"Look Mocha, don't go tripping, alright?"

"Or what? Huh, Marcus? Or what?" Mocha laughs out like a chick who is about to run big game and hangs up the telephone.

Man, you can never trust a big butt and a smile. I'm hoping she ain't one of them crazy chicks that be stalking brothers. Then again, she's probably just calling my bluff. But I can't chance it. I page Bone over and over until my fingers cramp.

I take the cordless out to the driveway and wax my car to keep my nerves straight. Bone calls back about a half hour later.

"What's going on player?" Bone asks breathing like he just ran a marathon. "Why you blowing my pager up like that? It better be serious. I had to pull over to call you. What's up?"

"Have you talked to Mocha?"

"Naw, what's up?"

"Man, your cousin is tripping. She's threatening to go to the concert tonight and tell Tyanne that I got with her."

"You got with Mocha, player?"

"Naw, man. We almost got down, but naw nothing happened. I guess that's why she mad at me. I don't know. I just need you to talk to her. She can't be going up to that concert lunching like that. You need to talk to her. I ain't having that."

"Alright, I'll talk to her man. Chill."

"This is serious man. Me and Tyanne trying to work our thing out and this is the last thing I need."

"Hmph. I can't believe she got you wrapped up. Man, Mocha been working married men over for years. She'll take your little wee wee and then blackmail you. That's her street game."

"What? You knew this and you hooked me up with her?" Bone was either retarded or just straight up didn't care nothing about me.

"You talking crazy now player," Bone says, "I hooked you up so Mocha could help you out at Champions. The last thing I thought is that you would get freaky wit' her. You slipping New Jack."

"I know man. Just talk to her, alright?"

"I said I would. Chill out."

"Alright. So what time are we meeting for you to get your money?"

"I have to make a stop on the way in. I guess I'll be through that way at around six."

"Six? Come on man, that's cutting it kind of close. The concert starts at seven."

"Man, I'm in Norfolk. It takes a few hours. I'll try to get

there earlier. Don't worry. You'll get to the concert on time."

"Yea, alright man." I say. "Don't forget to call that crazy cousin of yours either."

"Crazy is as crazy does. Later Forrest Gump." Bone laughs and hangs up the phone. I'm not laughing. And he wouldn't laugh either if he knew what I was capable of doing if Mocha didn't back off.

CHAPTER THIRTEEN
Tyanne

"Girl, I am so glad you are deciding to trust God. And you whipped it on him this morning, too? I'm scared of you!" Patrice laughs as she pulls the last of the curler rods from my hair.

"Ssshh! You're all loud." I wouldn't have told Patrice but she said she could tell something was up when I walked into the salon and the crinkles she usually sees in my forehead were replaced with a big glow and lots of blushing. Besides, I usually end up telling her everything anyway.

"Chile' please" Patrice says, "For this cause shall a man leave his father and mother, and shall be joined unto his wife and they two shall be one flesh!"

"Preach!" A woman I don't know yells as she looks up from a book she's reading. Others in the salon smile at Patrice as they are used to her shouting scripture verses and singing praises unto the Lord at any given time of the day.

"I can't tell you nothing," I just shake my head all the while blushing. It feels good to have joy again. It also feels good having a best friend who owns a salon and spa. Patrice had her staff treat me to a full body massage, make-up, manicure, pedicure and she put a whipping on my hair.

"You made me beautiful girl." I say and prance back and forth in front of the mirror.

"Oh, you were beautiful before you came in here woman." Patrice says, "I know one thing for sure. Marcus is going to be happy to see something other than that dumb ponytail."

"Sure, you're right!" I can't do nothing but laugh at Patrice. I hadn't had my hair done in God knows how long. With all that has been going on, the last thing I cared about was a hairstyle.

"Oh, before I forget." Patrice reaches down in her smock and hands me a small white box. "Just a little something I had made to let you know how proud I am of you. And to remind you to keep the faith, sistergirl."

"What is it?"

"Open it up and see!"

Patrice is always being so thoughtful. Inside the box lay a gold bracelet and a dangling charm with an inscription of Psalm 37:5, *'Commit thy way unto the Lord; trust also in him, and he shall bring it to pass.'* Patrice knew it was my favorite scripture. "Awww, Patrice. Thank you, girl."

"You know since you have decided to trust God, the devil will be busy right?" Patrice reminds me, "You just stand on the promises of God concerning your marriage and your family. God has Marcus and he has Tiffany. You have to believe that He is in control, alright? What I want you to do is quote that scripture every time you feel weak and watch the Lord strengthen your butt right on up!"

"Girl, don't have me in here crying and messing up my make-up."

"You go on and cry if you want to. You can touch that stuff up when you get home."

"Yea, but I can't do it like your make up lady did it." I say sniffling and laughing. "Please don't have me going to the concert looking like Count Dracula."

"You'll be fine, silly." Patrice says.

"Thanks lady." I embrace my sister from another mother. The big sister I never had and always wanted. "Now, you know I have to be at church early. Don't forget I'm bringing the kids over."

"Yes, I know, I know. You have told me a billion times. Just drop the kids off at my house. Melvin will be there. I'll be off in another hour. Go on. Go get yourself together."

"I love you girl." I hug Patrice and grab my things. "Bye everybody!" I yell and wave goodbye to the rest of the spa.

"See you tonight, Ms. Miller!" a young girl yells.

"Go bless His name, Minister!" another yells out.

With a send off like this, I can do nothing but give God all the praise. He's already moving. Tonight God is going to work a miracle and show Himself strong and mighty. I can feel it.

* * *

My heart dances when I pull up and see Marcus' car in the driveway all shiny and waxed. *Yaay God.* Obviously he's sticking around and getting ready for tonight. The shower is running as I climb the stairs to our bedroom. I'd already dropped the kids off at Patrice's and now I was having thoughts of jumping all over Marcus.

I remove my clothes and put on a head wrap so that I won't mess up my hair. I start to tip toe to the bathroom until I see what I see on the dresser.

Wads of money folded in rubber bands, thousands of dollars, money just like the money I exchanged for my life years ago. Me and my children had nearly lost our lives over drug money. Why in the world was this kind of money sitting in my house again?

I stand shocked and naked and stare at the money.

"Whoa. Hey sexy," Marcus says as he comes out of the bathroom drying off with his towel. "I didn't hear you come in. You came back for some of this good loving?"

I don't answer. I just stand shaking my head in disbelief. His eyes follow mine to the dresser.

"Before you start tripping, that's not mine."

"Marcus, don't lie to me. Whose is it then?"

"It belongs to Bone. I'm serious. I'm taking it to him later."

I sit on the bed in all of my nakedness and try to make sense of it all. I want to believe Marcus but this is too much. All the memories from the past begin to flood my mind. I can't believe this is happening. "Marcus, do you realize what seeing this does to me? Are you that selfish and money hungry that you would risk the lives of your family? What is wrong with you?"

"Come here." He grabs me and pulls me close to him. Holding my face in his hands, he says, "Look at me. I swear on my grandmother's grave... "

"Marcus, you don't have to swear on your grandmother's grave."

"No, listen to me. I want you to believe me and I want you to hear me. I swear I'm not in the game anymore. I'm not selling. I'm not doing any more favors. Nothing. I'm done. I'm taking Bone his money and I'm going to let him know I'm out completely. This is it."

I just look at him and say nothing.

"I'm serious Tyanne."

"I hope and pray you are serious Marcus. I really do."

"I am baby. I have never been more serious in all my life. I've been doing a lot of thinking lately. I don't know. I think part of me wanted to stay in the game to have a financial back up. Not that I'm selling or anything, but just being there for Bone made me feel like I still had some kind of connection. It might sound stupid, but I've just been in the game so long that it was hard to pull all the way out. Then I think about my sons. I don't want them growing up doing this. I'm done man. I mean it. I got too much lose. And I love you too much to lose you."

This... must... be... heaven. After Marcus kisses me deeply and passionately, I want to stay in this way for all eternity.

"I love you, Mrs. Miller."

"I love you, too Marcus Miller."

"By the way, do you know a man that goes to your church who wears a white suit, white hat and white shoes?" Marcus asks.

"What? A white suit, white hat, and white shoes?" I ask looking at Marcus like he's crazy. "What's his name?"

"That's what's crazy. I don't know. He came to the Hood Auditions. I looked at his info sheet and noticed he didn't write down his name. I do remember that he looks a little bit like Grady from Sanford and Son though."

"Grady? I have no idea as to whom or what you are talking about Marcus. Why? What happened?"

"Forget it. I can tell you are clueless. It's just that some guy came to the audition singing Jesus is Love. I thought you sent him."

"You thought I sent him? You ever think that God may have sent him?"

"Maybe God did, because I don't know anybody around here that would wear all that white like that. Baby, he had on white shoes *and* a white hat."

"Okay, Marcus. You made that clear." I want to laugh, but I hold it in. I need to take advantage of this intimate moment and be honest with the man I love more than anything. I press my head into his chest and allow the silence to consume the room once again before I speak. "I was going to leave you this weekend." I say in one breath.

"Leave like leave me, leave me?" He asks as he looks down at my face. I thought he would break away from our embrace, but he doesn't.

"Yes, I was going to leave you." I say looking up into his eyes. "But I decided I wanted our marriage more."

"What? You were going to leave all of this?" He says as he presses in harder against me.

"All what?"

"All this?" He presses against me harder once again and smiles.

"Yep, I sure was." I smile into his handsome, loving face, a face I haven't seen in this way in a long time. "But I love you so much Marcus. And I believe God has something for us."

"He does. He told me to give it to you right now." He leans me back onto the bed and at that moment the only thing that matters is making love to my man.

CHAPTER FOURTEEN
Marcus

I usually get a bad feeling about things and decide not to do them. Those feelings have saved me from death and jail many times throughout my time on the street. I start to tell Bone I can't meet him at the hotel, but since it's so close to Solid Rock Christian Center I figure I can just shoot on over to the church from there.

This time I had a bad feeling along with a terrible stomachache from some Chinese food I ate on the way. I knew when I ordered it, I would regret it, but unfortunately I had a Big Bone moment and decided I wanted to eat some grease and clog my arteries today. Well. I'm left with no choice but to have to hear Bone's mouth and stink up his hotel bathroom.

I park in the garage and catch the elevator to the seventh floor. I look for room seven thirty three, tap on the door a few times and wait for Bone to lift himself up. I know it takes him a few minutes to pull his big butt off the bed or wherever it is he's sitting.

"Yeah?" He mumbles through the door.

"Yeah." I answer. He knows my voice.

When he opens the door, he's talking on the telephone and holding a glass of something that will have him giggling all night. I step in and sitting in the chair is the last person I want to see smiling at me real wide holding a glass of wine. I can't believe Bone has Mocha here. I asked him to talk to her not set us up on a date. Bone be tripping.

Bone still talking on the phone, waves at me to help myself to the wine and platter of cheese and crackers he has on the table. I ignore him and turn up my lips.

"I can't believe you told Bone I was going to stalk your wife." Mocha says smiling with her crazy self.

"Look." I say with my hand pointed in her face." I don't play like that. You were about to get yourself hurt girl. You shouldn't play like that."

"Aw, come on gangster." Mocha jokes. "You wasn't about to hurt wittle 'ole me, was you?" Mocha stands up and rubs up against me.

I push her off. "Stop playing girl. What's wrong with you?" I give Bone a look that tells him to get off the phone. I was ready to give him the money and get out of there.

"Look, don't be pushing me," She says rolling her neck with her hand on her hip. I guess her little feelings were hurt since I wasn't giving into her little freaky stuff. "I'm only here because Christopher told me that I needed to come here so you and I could straighten our beef. I could care less one way or the other."

"Ok, you can call it a beef or whatever you want. But like I told you and Bone or Christopher as you like to call him, we need to squash whatever this is. I apologize for pulling you into something that was more complicated than I realized. I'm sorry for wrapping your feelings up like that."

"True that. True that. I guess I accept your apology." She says smiling and then runs her tongue across her lips. The more I look at her; I realize shortie is just lost and half crazy. All that sexiness I somehow imagined has disappeared, for real. I had her pegged wrong. I must have been one horny brother to let it get this far. I'm just glad Tyanne is back to her senses and I can get my goodies at home. Man, oh man.

"Cool. So we have an understanding, right?" I ask.

"Yes, we have an understanding." Mocha says and smiles. I unhook my belt and unzip my pants to pull out the money.

"Oh, so you wanna squash our beef by doing a little something, something?" Mochas asks. "Heyyyy! Ho! Even while Bone is in here? So you do have a little freak in you after all! Ha!" Mocha laughs and starts dancing around the room with her wine glass.

Obviously the wine is getting to her. She lied big time

when she said she didn't drink. Shortie be drinking like a fish. I just shake my head at her and unload the stacks of money from my underwear onto the bed.

"Hey man, what are you doing?" Bone says as he hangs up the telephone and stuffs some cheese and crackers in his mouth. "How you know I want Mocha to see how much money I got?"

"Either she sees it or it's about to get a lot of doo doo all over it. Man, that Chinese food I had tore my stomach up. Let me use your bathroom." My stomach starts rumbling like a volcano is about to erupt.

"Uh-huh. That's what you get talking about me! I thought you didn't eat that kind of food? You be faking. Man, don't go in there funking up the bathroom. Hold it until you get where you going. Nicole is on her way up, come on man!" Bone yells through the door. Now, I could care less about Pancake Butt smelling it.

"Hold it? Man, you done lost your mind! I ain't holding nothing!" I yell back. "They got spray in here! I'll take care of it, man!" I say laughing and yelling over the bathroom fan. I can hear Mocha out there cracking up. I lock the door and get comfortable. I knew I was going to be sitting there for a while.

"Guess who that was on the phone?" Bone yells through the door, "That was that dude Freddie. You remember Freddie Wilson from P Street? Yeah, that was him. He told me that he supposed to be moving to Atlanta next month. He said he's having him a big house built down there. I told him to check into some property out there for me. Never know man. I just might pack up and leave all you bammas!"

Bone can rap for hours when he's been drinking. And he don't need nobody to say uh-huh or nothing. He'll just keep rapping and rapping. I don't have a clue as to who Freddie Wilson is and Bone know good and well he ain't moving to no Atlanta. The farthest he's moving is from the couch to the refrigerator.

6:45 p.m. That's what time it is and I can't get up off the toilet. My stomach is killing me. There is no way I can be late for Tyanne's concert. Hopefully they will have prayer and do a whole bunch of talking and stuff before the actual concert starts. Church people never know how to get to the point no way.

I'm really proud of Tyanne. I haven't had a chance to tell her with everything that's been going on. Shoot, when she decided to whip it on me, I really didn't care about talking then. Then this situation with Tiffany has us all messed up. Tyanne is right. We still have lots of talking to do.

I thought I was tripping for a minute, but I know I heard the door slam, some fumbling around and the TV volume go up real loud. I reach up and cut off the fan switch so I can hear.

"Get on the floor!" I hear a voice yell and then more fumbling around.

"Who in the bathroom?" Another voice yells my way and starts banging on the door. "Open the door!"

What the...

"Alright, you don't have to open the door. I'll be in there!" The voice says. Just then I hear three muffled shots and Mocha screams. I know it's Bone. They took my man out cold-blooded.

"Shut up hoe!" The voice yells at Mocha.

I feel like I'm outside of my body. All I can do is stand there with my pants down, my mouth opened, eyes big. I have no where to run. No window. No nothing.

One of the dudes came back to the door and started banging again. "Open the door! Either open it up or I'm kicking it open!" I wasn't opening the door. I was either going to try to fit down into the toilet or the sinkhole but I wasn't about to open the door.

"Please, please don't shoot me! I beg you! Please don't shoot me!" I hear Mocha crying and begging.

"Didn't I tell you to shut up?" A voice yells and then I hear another gunshot. I listen for voices. I hear nothing but the television.

All of a sudden, dude starts banging up against the door again. I'm holding the door closed with my body as hard as I can. It's not working. I can feel the door giving in.

"Won't you go 'head, man! I ain't seen nothing!" I yell. Fear is sapping all of the energy out of my body. I'm shaking so hard, I can hardly breathe.

Just as I try to reposition my body on the door, dude kicks the door again. This time the door swings open and knocks me against the wall. All I see is the barrel of a nine millimeter and the face of my killer. My killer has a name though. It's Phil Perry.

"What's up player? If ain't ole party thrower himself?" Phil says. "Did big boy think he could just screw my girl and get away with it?"

Damn. This was about Bone screwing Pancake Butt. This dude is going to take me out and leave me for dead over some freak body. I see it in his eyes. I back into the shower, pulling the shower curtain, pole and everything with me. I raise my hands as high as I can and beg for my life. "Please man, don't shoot me. I got too much too lose... come on, main man... "

"Shut up punk" is all he has for me. My words mean nothing to him. I hear two gunshots and then all of a sudden I feel a burning pain shoot through my whole body. He cocks the gun for a third time.

"Come on, man." A dude yells from the front door. "I got the money. Let's go!"

"You go it?" Phil yells back never taking his eyes off me.

"Yeah, man. I got it. Come on!"

Things are getting blurry, but I can see Phil's legs as he runs out the door behind the dude. The pain is crazy. It feels likes my whole body is on fire. And the loud volume from the TV is making my head pound and hurt even worse. Every move I make hurts. Thinking hurts.

I'm not going out like this though.

I can't die like this.

I won't die like this.

With one arm, I pull myself out of the tub and crawl out to the room. I want to get to the phone, but the more I move, the worse the pain. I have to get to the phone... I need to call 9... I need to call 9... I can't move... I can't see.

Jesus, please help me... please don't let me die like this...

CHAPTER FIFTEEN
Tyanne

His seat is still empty. I've looked out in the sanctuary about a hundred times to see if Marcus has joined Patrice, Melvin and the kids but he is no where in sight. As much as I want to have an attitude about Marcus not being at the concert, as much as I cannot believe that Marcus is going to miss the most important night of my life, I know I have to let it go. In about sixty seconds, Nile will play my cue on the piano and I will walk out and begin singing with all my might unto the Lord.

I kneel down at the chair in the hallway and pray for me, our band, people who have come out to the concert, and Marcus – wherever he is. *Order his steps Lord.* I end my prayer in tears and whispers of Thank You Jesus.

I hear my cue. Wearing a yellow satin dress with a modest bodice and a-line cut and my new Tracy Reese, patent leather sling back heels, I walk out to the sanctuary and my heart skips a beat. It is standing room only. From one side of the room to the other, people are clapping, whistling and shouting praises unto God. The audience gives a standing ovation that must have lasted about ten minutes. I point to the heavens and the crowd claps and praises God even louder. Soon a joy and a peace fill my heart that no devil in hell can ever penetrate. I sing unto the Lover of my soul:

Lord, You are the light of my life
You are my sweet salvation
My heart sings for You
I give You full adoration

Nile, Russ, Boyd, Rick and Nakeeta play fiercely. We all look at one another and smile. It feels so right. The studio work can't begin to touch what God is doing through us live.

Everything is flowing. The sound system is glitch less. The music is flawless. People have their hands lifted; some clap and sway to the melody. It is altogether lovely.

"Ya'll feel alright tonight?" I ask the crowd.

The crowd responds with a resounding "Yeah!" Some shout hallelujah. Others just sit and bob their heads to the melody. The Spirit of God is in this place. God will not allow my heart to be sad for Marcus not being here. I am reminded at that moment that the night belongs to Him – my Beautiful and Wonderful Savior, Jesus Christ.

"We welcome you to the worship concert for our debut CD, 'Fresh Grace.' I'm Tyanne Miller. Please put your hands together for our incredible band... on violin, we have the beautiful and incomparable, Nakeeta Adams! On bass guitar, the talented yet crazy, Russ Joyner! Playing the saxophone, let's give it up for Slick Rick Roberson! On drums, we have Boyd 'Pretty Boy Floyd" Williams! And our spectacular maestro, the mastermind along with King Jesus, Solid Rock's own minister of music, with his bad piano playing self, let's give it up for Nile Rivers!" The crowd goes wild again.

"And we are... Windstorm."

Nile plays the piano with a surge of Holy Ghost Power and causes a sweet hush over the crowd. I close my eyes and harmonize:

Lord, You are, You are, You are, You are
Lord, You are, You are, You are, You are
Lord, You are, You are, You are, you are

As the band joins in, I open my eyes and look over again at the seat for a sign of Marcus. He's still not here. Just then I see Patrice, Melvin and the kids get up from their seats and leave the sanctuary. Why are they leaving?

There are times in your life when your faith in God is truly put to the test. I have no idea how I am going to get through five more songs, but I do. With the help of the Holy Ghost, I sing, scat and hum praises unto the Lord for all I'm worth. The musicians are lost in complete and total worship as they play seamlessly and beautifully. The audience, unaware of my inner turmoil, is enjoying every moment as they bob their heads and snap their fingers – every heart is on one accord.

When I sing, "As the Deer Panteth" I feel an incredible urge to cry unto the Lord. Overwhelmed by a feeling to open my mouth and call on the name of Jesus over and over, I can no longer sing in the key that we rehearsed. I begin to raise my hands and worship God – I surrender totally and completely. Without an inkling of how long I was worshipping, I open my eyes and see that more than half the sanctuary has their hands raised worshipping God. *Have Your way O Lord.*

"Sometimes you have to forget about protocol and let God know how much you love Him, amen?" The crowd claps and shouts in agreement.

We close out the concert with a jazzy remake of the Pace Sister's classic "U Know" and then I extend an invitation of salvation. That's when the incredible happens. When about fifty people trail to the front of the church and surrender their lives to the Lord, the congregation loses their mind. Glory to God! What a miraculous, marvelous night.

"Baby, you were fabulous!" Aunt Ruby says as she hugs and kisses me all over my face with her red lipstick. It is elbow room only in the lounge area as family and guests greet the band members. News cameras from various local stations are also there to gather footage for the evening news.

"Aunt Ruby, where did Patrice and the kids run off to?" I ask.

"They left? I didn't realize. Where were they sitting?" Aunt Ruby asks and then shifts her attention to one of her old church friends. She leaves me standing lost and totally confused. I have to find out what happened. Why did Patrice, Melvin and the kids leave all of a sudden?

Where did they go?

"Tyanne!" It's Nile grinning ear to ear. "Come with me. The photographer is ready to take pictures of the band and you my dear are being requested to sign CD's."

"Nile, do you know where Patrice and Melvin ran off

to?"

"No, I haven't seen them. Come on! This is your night my sister!" Nile says excitedly as he leads me to the table that is so beautifully set up with CDs and flowers. Behind the table sits a big poster sized picture of our CD cover. Windstorm: Fresh Grace.

It all seems like a hazy bittersweet dream. I'm standing here with a pasted smile and my mind left the building long ago. I can feel that something isn't right. I feel like I desperately need to be somewhere else. What is going on? Why doesn't anybody know anything?

As I force smiles for the photographer, I notice Aunt Ruby press through the crowd of people standing and staring at us take pictures. She waves at me to come to her. Her facial expression holds the unknown answers I'm looking for. Aunt Ruby knows something and my heart beats faster the closer I get to her.

"Come with me." Aunt Ruby says. Her face looks serious. "The police are here and they need to talk to you in Pastor's study." Aunt Ruby pulls my hand to follow her.

"What's wrong? What happened? "

Aunt Ruby keeps walking and says nothing.

CHAPTER SIXTEEN
Tyanne

In the study are Pastor, two detectives, me and Aunt Ruby.

"Mrs. Tyanne Miller?" The short one with the Wally Walrus moustache calls my name.

My expression begs him to get to the point. My heart can't take any more.

"I'm Detective Longhorn and this is Detective West. Your husband has been shot ma'am. He's in critical condition. We need you to help us by answering a few questions."

Shot? I shake my head in disbelief. My legs shake too and are on their way to collapsing until Aunt Ruby's arm holds me up and her strength demands I stand strong.

"Ma'am, what time did you last see your husband" The taller one with the baldhead asks.

"I don't know... this afternoon. Look, I need to get to my husband. I can't believe this... oh my God..." I start toward the door. "What hospital is he in?" I search the faces of both detectives.

"Ma'am, it will only take a moment." Wally Walrus says.

"I don't have a moment. I need to get to the hospital!"

"Minister Miller, calm down. It's okay," I hear Pastor's deep, reassuring voice say, "Answer their questions. We'll get you to the hospital. Don't worry."

"Pastor, with all due respect. I'm not answering any questions. I'm going to the hospital to see my husband. Excuse me." I say as I wait for Detective West to shift his body out from in front of the door before I move him myself.

"Officers, please," Pastor finally agrees. I guess he caught a peek at my balled up fists. "Maybe we can get these questions answered some other time. Minister Miller would like to get to the hospital to see her husband. Excuse us gentleman."

Wally Walrus gives me a card and says he will contact me later. I know Marcus is in some type of trouble with Bone, but I don't care about any of that. All I care about is getting to Marcus. I want to pray with him. Let him know I love him and everything is going to be alright. I only hope he remembered to call on the name of Jesus.

Pastor prays with me and Aunt Ruby before we leave and promises to let Nile know what's going on. I say a silent prayer in the car.

Lord, I know You as merciful and faithful God. I will trust You in all Your magnificent power to save my husband. Heal and comfort my husband O Lord. And Lord if You would, please let me get to Marcus and tell him that I love him, to tell him to hold on. Lord, please don't let my husband die. Save him Lord. Please save him.

* * *

When Aunt Ruby and I arrive at the hospital, the lady at the front desk tells me that Marcus is in surgery on the third floor. As I head to the elevator, Patrice, Summer and Lil Markie run up and hug me. Jordan is sound asleep in Patrice's arms. I thank God for friends who love you and are there when you need them. I don't know what I would have done had Patrice and Melvin not been around tonight.

"Thanks for being here." I say and kiss Patrice's cheek.

"Now where else would I be?" Patrice says, "One thing I do know. We're in the midst of a mighty move of God."

"How is he?"

"Marcus is fine." Patrice says. "Calm down Ty. Everything's going to be okay. There's nothing you can do at this point. Marcus is in surgery and you won't be able to see him for a little while. Melvin's up there praying and anointing everything in sight with oil. You know Deacon Mel is on it."

Just knowing that Melvin is up there interceding for his childhood friend makes me feel better, Although Marcus and

Melvin have grown apart, Patrice has shared with me that Melvin has never stopped praying for Marcus.

"Where's Tiffany?"

Patrice looks at me as if she has just come down from the Mount of Glory. "Come with me." Patrice gives Jordan to Aunt Ruby, asks her to keep an eye on the kids and leads me to the elevator. Once on the elevator, Patrice presses number two.

"I thought Marcus was on the third floor?"

"He is," Patrice says calmly. "We need to go to the second floor where Tiffany is." Patrice has a slight smile on her face which is odd for all that is going on. "Just as you started singing, Tiffany leaned over to me and told me she felt like she was bleeding. Sure enough, she was. Girl, the first thing that came to my mind was that God was doing a cleansing. I knew instantly what was happening. Baby girl was having a miscarriage. I tapped Mel on his lap and said to him, 'Come on and start praying.' Lord knows He was moving. So we get here at the hospital and we find out Marcus is here. We find that out while we're sitting in the waiting room watching a newsflash on TV. Mmph. All I could do was call on the name of Jesus."

I just shake my head. I'm both speechless and humbled. I'm torn between accepting what I thought would be and then having to instantly shift my emotions to what has manifest. God is definitely having the final say in all of this. I'm humbled and I'm speechless.

When we reach the entrance of Tiffany's room, I hug Patrice and we both praise and thank God over and over for His goodness, His grace and His mercy.

Patrice goes back to join Aunt Ruby and the kids. I walk into the room and see my baby girl, lying on the bed with a look that longs for a mother's embrace. Even so, she has a face that glows. Same round face with the braid extensions, but somehow she looks different to me tonight.

"Hi Ma," Tiffany says with tears forming in her eyes. As soon as I am close enough, she grabs me and hugs me tightly. I rub her head as she cries and releases all of the hurt and guilt that she's been carrying around for way too long. The Lord is purging and purifying my baby for sure.

"It's alright baby. It's alright," I say and kiss her cheek. "You're going to be just fine."

"I heard about Dad. Is he okay?"

"He's in surgery. He'll be fine. Just keep praying for him."

"I can't believe all of this is happening." Tiffany says, "And on the night of your concert."

"That's okay. This was the night it was supposed to happen."

"Ma, I'm done with this whole sex thing. I mean it." Tiffany says, grabs a tissue and wipes the tears from her eyes. "I know you may not believe me and I know I let you down, but I'm going to change. You just watch. I'm not letting the devil take me out like this."

Alright now. This was indeed new and bold talk that I've never heard coming from Tiffany's too-cool-to-praise-Jesus mouth. The Bible does say if we raise our kids up in the way they should go, when they are older they will not depart. I want so much to believe her, yet I know that will power alone won't do it. Tiffany will need to live the word and apply the word to her life. And I know she knows the word of God. Shoot, I raised her up in it.

"So help me God, I'm going to live my life totally for Him. I never want to go through anything like this ever again."

"And you don't have to, sweetheart. Just continue to remind yourself of how much of a beautiful diamond you are. You are worth the wait. Always know that God has major plans for your life."

"Are you mad at me?"

"Mad? No. Disappointed? Yes and I was even a little angry for a while. But right now I'm just thanking God that you're okay. That's the only thing that matters. I thank God that He had His way and you're okay."

"Pray with me Ma. I want you to stand with me as I recommit my life to Him."

"Father God," I start until I hear my daughter's voice overpower mine. Tiffany is leading the prayer. I yield to her prayer as I am sure Tiffany's voice is the one God is looking to hear at this moment.

* * *

After eating sinful snacks and falling asleep in the waiting room, an hour or so later I am awakened by a nurse telling me that I can go to Marcus' room. Patrice, who is sitting next to me, tells me that Aunt Ruby took the kids home as I slept.

I notice the waiting room is crowded with many of Marcus' friends and other people I don't recognize. They are huddled around whispering about what they heard and think they know. They must have seen the newsflash about Marcus on TV. As I head toward the elevator, I see Ms. Tilda, Marcus' mother coming off the elevator. I reach to hug her and she cries uncontrollably. As we embrace, I pray silently asking God to comfort her and lift me up on my most holy faith. I know what she's feeling, but I don't want Ms. Tilda's pain to break me. I'm determined to stand on the promises of God and believe that Marcus is going to be fine.

I could never prepare myself for what I was to see. When I walk into Marcus' room and I see the tubes coming out of his nose and the puffiness of his face, I'm unable to hold back the tears. I've never seen my husband in this way. I'm so used to seeing him standing tall and being strong. Even when he's unsure and afraid, Marcus will stick his chest out and pretend to be the boldest and baddest man alive. Seeing him tonight makes my heart hurt for him.

At this moment, I clearly understand about the one flesh scripture in the book of Matthew. The Bible tells us when a man leaves his father and mother and is joined to his wife, they become one flesh. When I sang at the concert, I felt an intense desire to cry out in worship. That could have very well been the same time Marcus was fighting for his life. And all I knew to do was fight with my voice. Not realizing that both our spirits were yearning as one.

As I walk to the bed, the nurse walks past me to the monitor sitting overhead. She pecks at the keyboard, looks at the computer monitor and then records what she sees onto her clipboard. She looks at me and says, "Oh, he's gonna be just fine, don't worry. He's a soldier. He was shot once in the abdomen and took another shot in the shoulder. And the shots were done at close range, too. Honey, he should be dead, but the man upstairs was truly looking out for him."

"Hmph, yeah, God was looking out for him for sure." I say with a slight emphasis on 'God.' Anyone who refers to our great and sovereign God as the man upstairs just doesn't have a clue. Bless her heart. I forgive her. I do let her know though, "And he has a praying wife, too."

"I know that's right." With that, the nurse smiles and leaves the room.

I am determined not to cry as I stand next to Marcus. I want so much to be strong for him. I want all of the big God and big faith I talk about to stand with me. I want my very presence to strengthen and encourage Marcus to hold on and survive. I realize that all of the complaining I'd been doing was only a distraction of the enemy. The devil had me focusing way too long on all that was wrong, instead of all that God is working out on my behalf. Tonight is a sign that God is taking our marriage, our family, my life to a whole new level. I want and need my husband to survive. I love him so much.

When I grab Marcus' hand, he squeezes it gently and tears roll down the sides of his cheeks.

"I love you…" I whisper into his ear and gently kiss his sweet, puffy lips. "God loves you too and He is going to save you."

Marcus squeezes my hand again.

I have a feeling everything is going to be alright.

"Oh… oh… oh… I've got a feeling everything is gonna be alright" I sing softly in his ear, "I've got a feeling everything's gonna be alright, be alright, be alright, be alright… "

ONE YEAR LATER
Tyanne

Champions Restaurant & Supperclub
February 13, 1994

"Alright, where are my married couples?" I ask the crowd standing before me. It's opening night of Second Sundays at Champions Nightclub – a Pre-Valentine's Day Celebration. Second Sundays is a venue for gospel artists and inspirational entertainment that Marcus claims he dreamt up, but I know the real deal. Marcus decided he would keep his original musical format on other nights, but he did get rid of the alcohol. Many of his regulars stopped coming when they learned alcohol wasn't being sold at the club. Good riddance. I've learned to stop worrying. God always knows the end from the beginning.

"I want all of the married couples in the house to stand to your feet. Come on. Don't be shy. Stand up and grab your partner's hand."

Giggles and jokes fill the room as everyone pushes back their chairs and stand to their feet. The building is filled to capacity along with Aunt Ruby, Patrice and Melvin who sit near the front. My sister Janelle even shows up with a guy I've never met before. I'm just glad to see her with anyone else other than her womanizing baby's daddy. My supervisor Darnell and his wife make it out, along with various church members, distant family, friends and even a handful of local celebrities. Wearing shades of reds, white and pink, the love in the air is thick and wonderful.

To my surprise, Marcus joins me on stage and presents me with a dozen yellow roses. I want to melt. The crowd goes wild with oohs, aww's and applause. It's such a lovely thing to have him so freely expressing his love for me. Marcus grabs me around my waist as both my hands are occupied with the microphone and the roses. I feel a little embarrassed at first standing like this in front of everyone, but then I'm thinking, shoot this is my husband!

"Alright everyone, look your soul mate in the eye and repeat after me, say baby..." I look into Marcus's eyes and he looks in mine and we both say to one another, "What God has joined together... we will never, ever let no man... no woman... .no kids... no bill collectors... no scandals... no nothing tear us apart... I will love you with all of my heart... mind... and soul... for all eternity... Happy Valentine's Day. You may now kiss your love." Marcus kisses me so deep and sensually, he makes me forget I'm on the stage before a room full of people with a microphone in my hand. That is until I hear claps and whistles from the audience as they look our way.

"Watch out there now, minister!" Russ yells out with his crazy self.

"Now, that faith confession was for the married folk," I say, "You recently engaged folk or those of you who call yourself going together, whatever that means, you'll get your chance!"

The crowd laughs. Some of the singles jokingly boo.

"Alright. Ya'll ready to have a good time?"

"Yeah!"

"Hallelujah!"

"We have a dynamic line up for you guys. Coming up later in the evening we'll have the beautiful saxophonist Angella Christie, the magnificent sounds of Ben Tankard, and to round out our evening, the fantastic and anointed, Kirk Whalum!" The crowd goes wild.

This is a dream come true. This past year my family and I have been tried through the fire and the water, but God has brought us to a wealthy place. Soon after Marcus was released from the hospital, he started going to church and eventually he stood before the congregation at Solid Rock and gave his life to Christ. He hasn't attended church every

Sunday, but he gave his life to Jesus Christ and that's what matters most. God will grow him up into the mighty man of valor that he's soon to be.

Overall, life is good. Tiffany is now involved with the youth ministry in the church and heads up an abstinence workshop. Lil' Markie is doing much better in school and is no longer fighting. Summer is preparing to compete in the Scripps National Spelling Bee.

The biggest test for me has been dealing with church folk. The story of Bone and Marcus hit the local newspapers as, "Local Minister's Husband Wounded in Drug Deal Gone Bad" which brought about an incredible challenge for me. Supposedly Marcus was the local Tony Montana and I was Elvira from Scarface. I've heard it all. But that's alright. You reap what you sow.

Even though Marcus was let off with a year's probation, I still had to deal with gossiping and backbiting in the church in unprecedented proportions. Folks questioned my position on the ministerial staff. Some even wanted me to leave the church. Others prayed for me and my family. I praise the Lord for Pastor Murphy's stance. Pastor made it clear that he supported me and my family and called those who condemned hypocritical Philistines.

Eventually, it all passed and the church began to refocus on the things of God. I surely thank God for God. My relationship with Him is the only thing that got me through and helped me to withstand the storm.

Speaking of storms, Windstorm's CD stayed on the gospel billboard charts for eight weeks in a row. That leap on the music charts prompted a tour with Kirk Whalum, plenty of magazine and TV interviews and a guest appearance on Bobby Jones Gospel.

The experience has been life-changing. And you better believe me, Nile, Russ, Nakeeta, Boyd and Rick have loved each and every minute of it. Finally, jazz or gospel jazz, whatever folk choose to call it, is receiving the attention it so very well deserve.

As for me and Marcus, our love continues to grow stronger and stronger as I continue to pray and trust God to grow Marcus up in the things of the Lord. And I never cease to thank God for where we are now.

Reading Group Guide
Discussion Questions

1. Tyanne is contemplating leaving her husband. Is her reason scriptural? If not, why? If so, quote the supporting scripture(s). Explain your answer.

2. You have met both Tyanne and Marcus. What opinions have you formed about them?

3. Tyanne talks about how she went through a period where anxiety attacks and depression overwhelmed her after the robbery. What scriptures do you turn to keep your spirit lifted during challenging times?

4. Tyanne manages Marcus' nightclub business? Is she wrong to do this? Why or why not? Is she being over-religious concerning the nightclub?

_____
_____
_____
_____
_____

5. The bible tells us in I Corinthians 7:3-5 let not the wife or husband defraud one another when it comes to his or her body. Tyanne denied Marcus lovemaking. Is it part her fault that Marcus gave into the sexual temptations of Mocha? Why or why not?

_____
_____
_____
_____
_____

6. Tyanne discovers that her daughter Tiffany is pregnant. Marcus wants her to have an abortion. Is she right for wanting her sixteen year old daughter to have a baby? Should each situation be unique when it comes to Christians becoming pregnant and having abortions? Why or why not?

_____
_____
_____
_____
_____

7. "Before that day, she was fun, outgoing and had a bit of adventure in her. But after that walk up to the front of the church that day, she changed a whole lot." Marcus reflects.

Do you agree that some Christian women lose their sexuality the more spiritual they become and jeopardize their marriages? Explain your answer.

_____
_____
_____
_____
_____
_____

8. "Tyanne, once you declared in your heart that you were done trying and that you were leaving Marcus, the enemy got busy. The devil is just doing what he does best. You? You're confused, back and forth and the enemy is having a field day. The word of God says that a double minded man is unstable in all his ways. You don't know what you want from one minute to the next Tyanne. You either want your marriage or you don't." Tyanne's girlfriend Patrice tells her. Do we create our circumstances based on what we say and how we think? Do you agree or disagree? Explain your answer.

_____
_____
_____
_____
_____
_____

9. Tyanne is the assistant minister of music at her church. Do you think she should be in this position considering what's going on in her personal life? Why or why not? Quote scripture to support your answer.

_____
_____
_____
_____
_____
_____

10. "As for me and Marcus, our love continues to grow stronger and stronger as I continue to pray and trust God to grow Marcus up in the things of the Lord. And I never cease to thank God for where we are now." Tyanne concludes. Are you content with where you are now? If God decides to never change that one thing you are believing Him for, could you live with that? Explain.

_____
_____
_____
_____
_____
_____

NEW NOVELS COMING SOON!

That Summer Morning

Barbara Jean Simmons vowed never to return to DC again after that unforgettable summer in '83. She caught a bus back home to Big Mountain harboring the dreadful secret of what happened the day of her eighteenth birthday. Unable to cope with the pain and guilt, Barbara Jean turned to a careless lifestyle of drinking, drugs and sleeping around with any man walking until God sent one of His angels to lead her to the road of reformation.

Nearly twenty years later, a saved and sanctified Barbara Jean returns for a week long trip to D.C. to perform the wedding ceremony for Cousin Valerie Ann's daughter, Noelle. However, there are others in the family who remember the shameful family secret and aren't impressed with the church robe and her so-called newfound Christianity. The memories of a haunting past overshadow the light Barbara Jean so desperately tries to shine as she is forced to face the demons she left behind.

Determined to win God's favor and prove her spiritual transformation to those who doubt, Barbara Jean realizes that it is her earnest faith and trust in God that will bring the ultimate healing, acceptance and true love that awaits her.

In Pursuit of Nappiness
(An excerpt)

Sylvia's mind raced as she drove her white, Chevy Yukon truck down the beltway with all the windows rolled down accelerating to eighty miles per hour. She dared a state trooper to try and stop her. He would just have to chase her because she wasn't about to slow down.

Sylvia cried out loudly from her truck window as the wind stroked her face and beat against the trash bags that lined the back seats. Blinded by her tears and the oncoming headlights of the other vehicles, Sylvia swerved down the exit, darted in and out of traffic until she pulled in front of the house.

Sitting motionless in a pair of jeans and her "Jesus Saves" sweatshirt, Sylvia stared at the door of 333 Edgewood Terrace. Everything inside of her wanted to run and kick the door in. Yet, the little sanity she had left managed to constrain her and forced her to calculate how she would approach the situation. The hurt Sylvia felt was so deep her body ached. She had cried past hurt. Tonight she was grieving.

Not quite a millisecond later, her mind told her that being rational had its place. But not tonight.

The bastard. How could he? I gave him twenty years of my life. For what? For this?

Sylvia climbed out of the truck and opened the back door. One by one, Sylvia grabbed the trash bags filled with clothes, shoes and other personal belongings and lined them on the curb. With sweat beads rolling down her forehead and tears streaming down her cheeks, Sylvia walked to the back of the truck and pulled out the hammer. She walked a few feet forward to the shiny, light blue Bentley coupe parked in front of her truck. Without hesitation, she began to bust out each window of the car.

❖ To purchase additional copies of this book, please visit www.Amazon.com. For information on other books and works by Sheritha Bowman, please visit www.sherithabowman.com.

Other Books by Sheritha:

Diary of a Woman Pastor
1-60034-752-5

E-mails for the Christian Soul: 102 Messages of Praise, Hope and Revelation
0-595-25427-6

This Too Shall Pass: Meditations, Affirmations and Encouragement for My Sisters
0-595-31565-8

Soul Inspiration: The Triumphant Testimony of a Praying Wife
0-595-20570-4

*Keep praying and believing
and thank you for your support!*

Sheritha Bowman